"Everything [Olsen] has written has become almost immediately a classic."—Robert Coles

"[*Tell Me a Riddle* is] enough to make [Olsen's] name a truly important one in writing. . . . She can spend no word that is not the right one."—Dorothy Parker

For presentation of the Robert Kirsch Lifetime Achievement Award in 2000, literary critic Julian Moynihan wrote: "[Olsen] explores the deep pain and real promise of fundamental American experience in a style of incomparable verbal richness and beauty. As a great work of literary art [*Tell Me a Riddle*] will be read as long as the American language lasts."

In presenting Olsen with an award for her distinguished contribution to American literature, the American Academy and Institute of Arts and Letters cited her writing as "very nearly constituting a new form of fiction."

In citing Olsen's work for the 1994 REA Award, the jurors Charles Baxter, Susan Cheever, and Mary Gordon said, "With her collection, *Tell Me a Riddle*, Tillie Olsen radically widened the possibilities for American writers of fiction. These stories have the lyric intensity of an Emily Dickinson poem and scope of a Balzac novel. She has forced open the language of the short story, insisting that it include the domestic life of women, the passions and anguishes of maternity, the deep, gnarled roots of a long marriage, the hopes and frustrations of immigration, the shining charge of political commitment.

Her voice has both challenged and cleared the way for all those who come after her."

"[Tillie] had invented a literary tradition of her own. . . . Every line is measured, compressed, resonant, stripped bare, so that paragraph after paragraph achieves the shocking brevity and power of the best poems. . . . By now I have read *Tell Me a Riddle* so often that it is essentially memorized."—Scott Turow, on National Public Radio's *You Must Read This*

TELL ME A RIDDLE,
REQUA I,
AND OTHER WORKS

TILLIE OLSEN

Foreword by Laurie Olsen

Introduction by Rebekah Edwards

UNIVERSITY OF NEBRASKA PRESS : LINCOLN

© 2013 by the Tillie Olsen Trust

Foreword and introduction © 2013 by the Board
of Regents of the University of Nebraska

Acknowledgments for the use of previously
published material appear on page 165, which
constitutes an extension of the copyright page.

Library of Congress Cataloging-in-Publication Data
Olsen, Tillie.
[Works. Selections]
Tell me a riddle, Requa I, and other works/
Tillie Olsen; foreword by Laurie Olsen;
introduction by Rebekah Edwards.
pages cm
Includes bibliographical references.
ISBN 978-0-8032-4577-8 (pbk.: alk. paper)
1. Working class—United States—Fiction.
2. Working class—United States—Social condi-
tions—20th century. 3. Olsen, Tillie. 4. Women
authors, American—20th century—Biography.
I. Olsen, Laurie. II. Edwards, Rebekah. III. Title.
PS3565.L82A6 2013
813'.54—dc23   2013002054

Set in Scala by Laura Wellington.
Designed by Ashley Muehlbauer.

CONTENTS

FOREWORD
Laurie Olsen

It is now over a century since Tillie's birth and nearly a decade since her death at age ninety-four, but, dear reader, I know that this meeting—this act of you picking up her book—would mean the world to her. By reading her stories now, in this twenty-first century that is so vastly different from the 1912 Nebraska farm world into which she was born, you give new life to her words. You are participating in a human chain that was core to Tillie's being—the relationship between writers and readers, those who write and those who read their stories.

Tillie's desk, workspace, and kitchen were crowded with photos of the faces of writers whose lives and writing touched her deeply. Passages from their books, letters, and journals were typed by Tillie onto blue scraps of paper and taped on bulletin boards, the edges of bookshelves, the refrigerator door, and the bases of lamps. Their faces and their words were her companions across generations, continents, and life circumstances: Olive Schreiner, Walt Whitman, Agnes Smedley, Herman Melville, Anton Chekov, Richard Wright, Franz Kafka, Emily Dickinson, William Blake, Thomas Hardy, Virginia Woolf, James Baldwin, Catherine Mansfield, W. E. B. DuBois, Zora Neale Hurston, Audre Lord, Adrienne Rich, and many dozens more spanning hundreds of years of writing and experience (some famous, some long-forgotten, some new unknown writers).

For Tillie, the writers who moved her soul were those whose lives and words bore witness to the drive to create—breaking through barriers of class, gender, mental illness, anti-Semitism, racism. The faces and words of her beloved writers were her life companions as fully as the downstairs neighbors, her family, and friends. She posted photos of their homes, their desks, the moor outside the Brontës' home, and Keats's chair. Tillie tucked their photos into envelopes to carry with her when she traveled and carried their quotes on slips of paper wherever she went, quoting them in conversations and in formal lectures, and even in delirium as she lay dying, intoned bubbles and fragments from her beloved writers.

Many of these inspirers were little-known or forgotten out-of-print writers, discovered by Tillie over years of exploring public library stacks and browsing in used bookstores. Tillie worked to bring their literature back to life. For Tillie, out-of-print literature was a loss for readers, and a kind of death for a writer. That's why, for our family, this centennial collection making her writing available anew means so much.

As a reader, Tillie felt great affinity for other readers. She was first and always a reader—hungry to talk about books, exchange books. She treasured her readers, and she thirsted for the company of other writers. It was the power of the written word that she experienced as a reader that inspired (Tillie once said "incited") her to become a writer. After readings, Tillie spent hours talking to people who came to ask her questions or request an autograph. The stories of their lives, their struggles, and their dreams poured out. Tillie evoked that kind of response from people and was deeply moved and honored by it. After Tillie's death, we poured through boxes and boxes of letters from readers all over the world bearing testimony to how Tillie's writing, Tillie's characters, Tillie's own life connected to their own life circumstances. She had developed correspondence with hundreds of readers and writers—building close friendships through letters with people she never had an opportunity to meet in person, friendships forged out of a shared love of literature.

As you read her stories now, try to imagine. If Tillie were alive, she would reach for your hand and hold it, touch your shoulder. Fixing her eyes on your face, she would want to know about you. And in careful listening, Tillie would urge you to write. To bring to literature what is not there now. To see the lapses and gaps in what makes it into literature and to add your own story and voice to written form. In her experience, it was those very gaps and invisible lives that convinced her she had something to contribute. "Visibility creates reality," she would say. It was her own struggle to be a writer against the odds and circumstances of poverty, her attention to human need, and motherhood that evoked a fierce determination to encourage others to find, believe in, and protect their impulses to write. With urgency, intensity, and belief she would say to you: "You, too, must write."

Reader, writer, or both—may you read and share this book with others. There is no greater gift to Tillie's legacy than the renewed life to her writing that you give by reading her stories and by carrying forward the compact between readers and writers into a new century. For that, thank you.

INTRODUCTION
Rebekah Edwards

This collection brings together Tillie Lerner Olsen's reportage writings from and about the 1930s along with her short fiction—the stories of the collection *Tell Me a Riddle* and the first part of what was to be a novella, "Requa I." This sampling of Olsen's writing allows us imaginative entry into the lifeworlds she recorded so faithfully and with such careful craft; it also documents some of the social conditions that motivated her work. The breadth and scope of this collection offers us a glimpse of Olsen's development from a young activist to a mature fiction writer to a writer at the end of her life looking back on a time that shaped her. The people recorded, enlivened, and imagined in these writings astound and challenge and inspire; they may simultaneously break our hearts and offer us solace.

Olsen was uncompromising in her belief that we must make a world in which "full humanhood" is possible, a world in which human dignity and the full development of people's capacities are cherished and nurtured. She was fierce in her insistence that people working together for social justice would make this world possible. At age eighty-three, she wrote in "A Vision of Fear and Hope" (first published in *Newsweek* in 1994 and now reprinted in this collection) that she still had hope. It was "beleaguered, starved, battered," and tested, yes, but hope still prevailed. In fact, she had "more than hope: an exhaustless store of certainty, vision, belief." Her conviction that change was possible stemmed, she said, from the radical social movements of the early twentieth century and all they accomplished, particularly in the 1930s, and it was sustained by subsequent decades of witnessing people working together for change. This certainty is at the heart of her writing.

Olsen has been cited for bringing people—working people who hadn't often been the subject of fiction—into literature through experimental forms of narrative: stream-of-consciousness and points of view that swerved from character to character to authorial address to quotations of songs, poetry, and political rhetoric. Olsen used the page, the line, the word in ways that were more expected in poetry than prose, in ways that have been described as "very nearly constituting a new form of fiction."[1] The results of such experimentation may be demanding to read, requiring readers to engage fully, to work, to participate in making the text's meaning. Her stories move readers deeply; it is not uncommon to hear people say they reread Olsen's work again and again.

Olsen was a writer who listened to how people said things, jotting down idioms, phrases, and slang on whatever was at hand, over the years piling up hundreds of scraps of paper scribbled with vernacular. She was a writer for whom every word had to be exactly right in connotation, cadence, and placement. In 1961 Dorothy Parker said about the stories in *Tell Me a Riddle* that Olsen could "spend no word that was not the right one." It was this resolute commitment to craft that resulted in work that would be cited for having "the lyric intensity of an Emily Dickinson poem and the scope of a Balzac novel."[2]

Olsen's experiments with language, the lives she brought into literature, and her visionary certainty succeeded in changing a piece of the world. Her work brought to the forefront literature that spoke to what Olsen called the "lives of most of us," literature that intervened in and broadened the traditional canon of texts by and about the privileged few. Her critical/theoretical work, published in 1978 as the book *Silences*, offered foundational concepts to the fields of women's studies, feminist theory, and American studies—and in doing so helped to change not only what kind of literature is taught in schools but how it is taught, and how it is considered in critical discourse.

A biography of Olsen's life can be found at the end of this collection. What follows here is a brief introduction to the works gathered in this volume.

TELL ME A RIDDLE

The book *Tell Me a Riddle* (1961) is made up of the short stories "I Stand Here Ironing" (1956), "Hey Sailor, What Ship?" (1957), and "O Yes" (1957), as well as a novella, "Tell Me a Riddle" (1960). Both "I Stand Here Ironing" and "Tell Me a Riddle" were included in *Best American Short Stories* the year they were first published, and "Tell Me a Riddle" won the O. Henry Award in 1961. These stories have been translated in many languages, anthologized widely, and have been made into films, staged productions, and an opera.

The stories of *Tell Me a Riddle* are linked by characters from different generations of the same extended family and by themes that "celebrate the endurance of human love and of the passion for justice, in spite of the pain inflicted and the capacities wasted by poverty, racism, and a patriarchal social order."[3] In these narratives, Olsen makes use of stream-of-consciousness, nonlinear chronology, an authorial voice that appears and disappears, a reliance on the cadence of vernacular speech, multiple points of view, and a poetic use of the word, the line break, and the page. Olsen's prose style in these works has been described as constituting "a literary tradition of her own . . . a narrative technique that [is] revolutionary . . . every line is measured, compressed, resonant, stripped bare, so that paragraph after paragraph achieves the shocking brevity and power of the best poems."[4]

Olsen's narrative structures in these stories are not, however, simply exercises in formal innovation. Rather, her form is intricately linked to the larger themes of the collection, and it is this relationship between the lives about which Olsen writes and the form she develops to do so that in 1961 caused the *London Times* to state in its review of the collection, "Out of poverty and hardship . . . [Olsen] reveals with compression, depth and a passionate economy of language a working class America that few writers have known or realized existed."

"I Stand Here Ironing," the first story of the collection, is a searing and nuanced take on motherhood and mother-daughter relationships and on the various influences that support or limit a child's full development of her capacities. Written as a mother's single, sustained monologue, it interrogates and makes vivid the difficulties faced by working-class women in the United States through the mother's consideration of how the economic poverty—the "want"—that her daughter Emily has grown up in has impacted both of their lives. The story ends with the mother's protective and fierce wish that Emily's sense of her value and agency somehow transcend the circumstances of her childhood: "Only help her to know—help make it so there is cause for her to know—that she is more than this dress on the ironing board, helpless before the iron."

Set in the 1950s, "Hey Sailor, What Ship?" moves in and out of the consciousnesses of an aging merchant marine, Whitey, and the members of the family of Helen and Lennie. Their friendship was formed in the 1930s as they organized the San Francisco waterfront. Over the years Helen and Lennie's family had become a refuge for Whitey to come home to between shipping-outs. In his latest visit, Whitey arrives drunk and collapses from illness, his body worn down by harsh working conditions and by the progression of his alcoholism. In "Hey Sailor, What Ship?" the idioms and songs of the waterfront, the rhetoric and vision of that earlier time of political activism, the shifting points of view, and the spacing and line breaks on the page combine to produce a potent form of narrative elegy. It is a story of loss—not simply one man's loss and increasing alienation but the loss of an earlier time when the united struggle for better working conditions and for a better world brought these people together.

"O Yes" is largely told from the perspective of Helen, who mourns as she watches her white daughter grow increasingly estranged from her best friend, who is black. As the two girls approach adolescence, they are forced apart by the formal and informal tracking of the American public school system of the 1950s, and by the systematic racial segregation that it supports. Writing largely in stream-of-consciousness and relying on the phrasing and music of a church baptism, Olsen renders the complexities and urgencies of embodied feeling, the politics that imbricate them, and the necessity and fragility of friendship as both inescapable and redemptive. Helen observes, "*It is a long baptism into the seas of humankind, my daughter. Better immersion than to live untouched.*"

At the center of the novella "Tell Me a Riddle" are the passions and conflicts within the long marriage of David and Eva. Their marriage had been formed during a time of political upheaval, and they had shared a revolutionary vision that a more just and humane world could be brought into being, a vision now tested by a life of poverty and hardship. David and Eva have become estranged and furious with each other, their conflicting needs tearing them apart; a lifetime of caring for children and husband has left Eva craving solitude while David craves sociability and companionship. The concerns of the novella are many: the tenacity and complexity of familial and marital love, the tasks and costs of motherhood, the marginalization of women, the experience of immigration, the increasing difficulties of aging and illness, the process of dying, the passion for justice that remains even in the face of all that is harmed and wasted by poverty and oppression. Written from multiple perspectives and using the rhythms of a Yiddish-inflected English, the structure of the novella offers a representation that Scott Turow has described as "more tender and affirmative than . . . grim . . . of how life can slaughter love."

It is about the dignity of values and the intense network of beliefs that ultimately connect humans to each other as they approach the end."[5]

The stories that make up *Tell Me a Riddle* testify to the urgent need to make a world in which these characters might be granted "full humanhood." When in the hospital, Eva insists that an identification form be changed: "Tell them to write: Race, human; Religion, none." It is a telling moment, sparsely written, one that illuminates Eva's revolutionary commitment to a future world that would not be structured by the inequalities and prejudices of racism, religion, class, and gender. One reads in the fierce, insistent cadence of Eva's demand the whole history of her belief—how it has been tested and battered but has sustained. It is a moment when we can see Olsen's commitment to conveying the full humanness of the people in her stories, to writing people into literature in ways that would make them recognizable to those who had never met them and recognizable to those close to them who had never seen them represented. These stories, and the passion, precision, and respect with which Olsen has written them, are a form of justice the lives of these characters insist we must call into being.

"REQUA I"

"Requa I," the opening of what was to be a novella, was published in the *Iowa Review* in 1970 and was included in *Best American Short Stories* in 1971. It is Olsen's most complex work, one in which the narrative style and what Elaine Orr has called the "redemptive hope" of the earlier fiction are brought to a new level of nuance and interrelation.[6] Olsen materializes the loss, disorientation, and fragmentation that are central concerns of the piece through the use of line breaks, words scattered across the page and justified to different margins, and a refusal of punctuation and closure. (The final word of the piece is not followed by any mark.) Olsen utilizes the vernacular of a poor and rural Northern California in the 1930s, while she also turns to poetic devices of alteration, assonance, and consonance to render the sounds not only of a people and of a time but of a place.

Requa is the name of a small, unincorporated town on the Klamath River in Northern California. It is an Anglicization of "Rekwoi," the Yurok name for the place. Olsen heard in its sound invocations of the words "requiem" and "reclamation," both of which are thematic concerns of this piece.[7] "Requa I" can be a hard piece to grasp because its characters and vernacular are unfamiliar to most readers, because of the difficulty of its narrative structure, and also because, as the first part of a longer work, it does not follow a traditional story arc—it does not resolve. The manuscript of the second part of "Requa" has been lost, and there is no record of how Olsen intended to develop and conclude this story. However, the piece itself, so formally and thematically concerned with the fragment, and with the reclamation of wholeness from brokenness, argues that wholeness exists not despite of or outside of the fragment, the broken, the unfinished but rather within the act of rendering something whole. It is the story's emphasis on the tenacity of human endurance, regeneration, and creativity that underscores Elaine Orr's suggestion that in "Requa I" "Olsen . . . insists . . . that brokenness is the condition that elicits human bondedness" and that "the story may await not so much Olsen's finishing of it as readers' response."[8]

"Requa I" is the story of Stevie, a thirteen-year-old boy emotionally shattered by the death of his mother and taken by his uncle Wes from San Francisco, the city he has grown up in, to Requa, an unfamiliar, rugged, small town in the Northern California redwoods. It is the story, also, of his uncle's commitment to care for Stevie, a care he understands to be not only material but psychic: "I'll help you to catch hold . . . I promise I'll help." This is a promise tremendously difficult to keep because Stevie has so completely withdrawn from human interaction—"(*No smile. Skinny little shrimp. Clutching at the door knob, knuckles white, nostrils flaring. Funny animal noises in his throat.*)"—and because of the struggle for daily livelihood they face in a time when "half the grown men in the county's not working." "Requa I" touches on many of the conditions and contradictions of the 1930s, not the least of these being the racism of the period. Olsen juxtaposes Stevie's thought "But they weren't ladies, they were Indians" to the racially mixed boarding house in which he lives, where whites, "Indians," and Chinese share the dinner table, a table that might be read as a prophetic metaphor, a vision of a future time when racism will no longer be tenable.

Written in a limited omniscient perspective, the text swerves between the consciousnesses of Stevie and Wes, often in the same paragraph, occasionally in the same sentence, leaving it to readers to identify who it is they are reading. There are times when this shift occurs with a description of the landscape, and then it is as if we are within the consciousness of Requa itself. Largely, however, the narrative is structured by Stevie's grief and the physical disorientation he experiences from his loss of parent and place. Stevie negotiates his loss defensively: "*Keep away you rememorings   slippings   slidings   having to hold up my head   Keep away you trying to get me's.*"

Stevie's grief begs healing, a healing that will come as a suturing of his fracturedness, as a wholeness forged through connection to place, to family, to community. It is a healing that takes place slowly, through a deepening connection to his uncle and to the land around him. It is a healing that comes from working in a junkyard, sorting the things that have been destroyed, cast off, abandoned. As he works, Stevie's own brokenness is inseparable from that of the junk, and along with the junk it is sorted through to see what is salvageable, what can be repurposed and put to use.

"Requa I" is the only one of the stories collected here that is set in the 1930s, a period that was so formative for Olsen as an activist and as a writer. As such, and as her final piece of fiction, it offers a powerful continuity between the stories of *Tell Me a Riddle* and her 1930s reportage work. We can see in "Requa I" a maturation of the experimental narrative techniques explored in the reportage and later developed in the fiction. "Requa I" also offers a sustained and nuanced account of the impact of the conditions of the 1930s, both the crushing economic and political climate and the vision of hope and certainty forged through human care for each other.

REPORTAGE FROM AND ABOUT THE 1930S

Olsen published "The Strike," "Thousand-Dollar Vagrant," and "I Want You Women up North to Know" in 1934 (her name then was Tillie Lerner). These pieces of experimental journalism are the work of a young writer whose subject matter and formal concerns were deeply intertwined with and influenced by the alchemical political and aesthetic movements of her time.[9] In her piece "A Vision of Fear and Hope" Olsen describes the sense of urgency and accomplishment of that period, the struggle for and aspiration to "not only 'the right to life, liberty and the pursuit of happiness' but the establishment of the means—the social, economic, cultural, educational means to give pulsing, enabling life to those rights." Olsen meant to "give pulsing, enabling life" to the events she recorded, writing in a way that would educate her readers and move them to action. Joseph Entin suggests that Olsen's writing during the thirties belongs to the genre of proletarian reportage; he describes this genre as a form of "engaged journalism" or a type of "modernist documentary," one in which literary experiment, journalistic account, and didactic call for action are inextricably joined.[10] At the National Writers Conference of 1935 (which Olsen attended), Joseph North described proletarian reportage as "three-dimensional reporting . . . both an analysis and an experience, culminating in a course of action."[11] As such, the form itself called into question the "objectivity" of mainstream journalism, throwing into relief the unacknowledged biases of those accounts and highlighting the ways in which political and social power is based in the ability to control how (and what) "reality" is represented. Yet, access to the means to control that representation is often reliant on political and social status.

Published in the *Partisan Review*, "The Strike" is an account of the 1934 West Coast Waterfront Longshoremen's Strike, specifically the events of "Bloody Thursday," when police fired into a crowd of strikers, wounding many and murdering two. The San Francisco longshoremen's strike lasted eighty-three days and eventually led to the unionization of all of the West Coast ports of the United States. "The Strike" utilizes collage and quotation, parataxis, surrealist imagery, and a passionate authorial voice that clearly states Olsen's positionality. Olsen's account works against the "objective," highly sensational attempts to frame the strike from a mainstream press owned by corporate and political "bosses." Olsen does this by placing her own impassioned experience at the center of her report, by juxtaposing inflammatory and antiorganizing headlines from the newspapers with her own bitter commentary, and by stating clearly that her goal is to move her readers, to write the piece "so that the beauty and heroism, the terror and significance of those days, would enter your heart and sear it forever." Olsen asserts that this is a piece written hastily, urgently: "Forgive me that the words are feverish and blurred. . . . But I write this on a battlefield"; it is a piece she insists is incommensurate to the importance of the events that have taken place, a piece left incomplete, to be considered and "written some other time" because "there is so much happening now."

"Thousand-Dollar Vagrant," published in the *New Republic*, is the account of Olsen's arrest during the longshoreman's strike when police raided an apartment that she was working in with other organizers. The charge of "vagrancy" was frequently used by the police when they wanted to arrest activists and could carry a fine of a thousand dollars. Anyone could be charged as a vagrant if they didn't have an address, a family who would take them in, or a job. The police would ask for that information, but the consequences for revealing it were so severe that most activists would not do so. According to Olsen, "If you give any names of members of your family they see that they lose their jobs; if you give your address they raid the place and wreck the furniture in the process of 'searching.' And even if you do show your 'visible means of support'—you're still a vagrant." The narrative is written as a direct, first-person account, and it is stylistically marked as reportage by its use of direct address to the reader, character sketches, dialogue and scene, and its didactic deployment of sarcasm and humor.

The poem "I Want You Women up North to Know" fits within the larger generic category of proletarian reportage in that it engages literary experiment, journalistic account, and didactic call to action. Constance Coiner suggests that "I Want You Women up North to Know" is an example of "worker correspondence poems," in which writers would take inspiration from letters written by workers and sent to newspapers and journals such as the *Daily Worker* or the *New Masses*.[12] This poem is based on a letter written by Felipe Ibarro (*New Masses*, 1934) condemning the owners of the Juvenile Manufacturing Corporation in San Antonio, Texas, for their exploitation of their workers. The poem uses many of the specific names and details included in the letter while Olsen "parodies a long bourgeois tradition of 'romanticizing' the worker."[13]

In Olsen's final piece of reportage, "A Vision of Fear and Hope," published more than fifty years later, we see a maturation of the techniques she used in her earlier work. This too is a piece of "three-dimensional reporting," in which experience and analysis are part of a larger imperative to educate and move the reader to action. The thirties Olsen remembers in this piece have much in common with our current times. Olsen writes, "One of every four farms was foreclosed, and half a million farm families lived at starvation levels." She cites Roosevelt's warning that "private enterprise is ceasing to be free enterprise" and his point that "1 percent of the nation's corporations were taking 50 percent of the profits." The similarities between that time and this are also invoked when Olsen describes the actions people took in response to those circumstances, actions both spontaneous and planned, actions that grew into movements: "stopping the evictions, putting the furniture back, on the picket lines, on the road, the pondering, questioning faces; the anguish not beaten." Olsen's reportage maintains the vision of a time when "the country was transformed by the hopes, dreams, actions of numerous, nameless human beings, hungry for more than food." These pieces urge us toward a certainty in hope, just as they encourage us to join with others to bring about a world in which "full humanhood" is possible.

NOTES

1. The American Academy and Institute of American Arts and Letters, Distinguished Contributions to American Literature Award statement, 1975.

2. Rea Award for Distinguished Contribution to the Short Story statement, 1994.

3. Deborah Silverton Rosenfelt, "From the Thirties: Tillie Olsen and the Radical Tradition," in *Tell Me a Riddle: Tillie Olsen* (New Brunswick: Rutgers University Press, 1995), 13.

4. Scott Turow, "Tillie Olsen's Tender Portrait of a Marriage," *All Things Considered*, NPR, November 7, 2006, http://www.npr.org/templates/story/story.php?storyId=6407142.

5. Turow, "Tillie Olsen's Tender Portrait."

6. Elaine Orr, *Tillie Olsen and a Feminist Spiritual Vision* (Jackson: Mississippi University Press, 1987), 121.

7. Orr, *Tillie Olsen*, 136n2.

8. Orr, *Tillie Olsen*, 121.

9. For discussions of Olsen's work in the context of the political and aesthetic movements in the United States in the 1930s, see: Constance Coiner, *Better Red: The Writing and Resistance of Tillie Olsen and Meridel Le Sueur* (New York: Oxford University Press, 1995); Joseph B. Entin, *Sensational Modernism: Experimental Fiction and the Photography in Thir-*

ties America (Chapel Hill: University of North Carolina Press, 2007); Rosenfelt, "From the Thirties."

10. Entin, *Sensational Modernism*, 151.

11. North as cited in Entin, *Sensational Modernism*, 151.

12. Coiner, *Better Red*, 161.

13. Coiner, *Better Red*, 162.

Short Fiction

TELL ME A RIDDLE

For my mother
1885–1956

I STAND HERE IRONING

I stand here ironing, and what you asked me moves tormented back and forth with the iron.

"I wish you would manage the time to come in and talk with me about your daughter. I'm sure you can help me understand her. She's a youngster who needs help and whom I'm deeply interested in helping."

"Who needs help." Even if I came, what good would it do? You think because I am her mother I have a key, or that in some way you could use me as a key? She has lived for nineteen years. There is all that life that has happened outside of me, beyond me.

And when is there time to remember, to sift, to weigh, to estimate, to total? I will start and there will be an interruption and I will have to gather it all together again. Or I will become engulfed with all I did or did not do, with what should have been and what cannot be helped.

She was a beautiful baby. The first and only one of our five that was beautiful at birth. You do not guess how new and uneasy her tenancy in her now-loveliness. You did not know her all those years she was thought homely, or see her poring over her baby pictures, making me tell her over and over how beautiful she had been—and would be, I would tell her—and was now, to the seeing eye. But the seeing eyes were few or non-existent. Including mine.

I nursed her. They feel that's important nowadays. I nursed all the children, but with her, with all the fierce rigidity of first mother-hood, I did like the books then said. Though her cries battered me to trembling and my breasts ached with swollenness, I waited till the clock decreed.

Why do I put that first? I do not even know if it matters, or if it explains anything.

She was a beautiful baby. She blew shining bubbles of sound. She loved motion, loved light, loved color and music and textures. She would lie on the floor in her blue overalls patting the surface so hard in ecstasy her hands and feet would blur. She was a miracle to me, but when she was eight months old I had to leave her daytimes with the woman downstairs to whom she was no miracle at all, for I worked or looked for work and for Emily's father, who "could no longer endure" (he wrote in his good-bye note) "sharing want with us."

I was nineteen. It was the pre-relief, pre-WPA world of the de-pression. I would start running as soon as I got off the streetcar, running up the stairs, the place smelling sour, and awake or asleep to startle awake, when she saw me she would break into a clogged weeping that could not be comforted, a weeping I can hear yet.

After a while I found a job hashing at night so I could be with her days, and it was better. But it came to where I had to bring her to his family and leave her.

It took a long time to raise the money for her fare back. Then she got chicken pox and I had to wait longer. When she finally came, I hardly knew her, walking quick and nervous like her father, looking like her father, thin, and dressed in a shoddy red that yellowed her skin and glared at the pockmarks. All the baby loveliness gone.

She was two. Old enough for nursery school they said, and I did not know then what I know now—the fatigue of the long day, and the lacerations of group life in the kinds of nurseries that are only parking places for children.

Except that it would have made no difference if I had known. It was the only place there was. It was the only way we could be together, the only way I could hold a job.

And even without knowing, I knew. I knew the teacher that was evil because all these years it has curdled into my memory, the little boy hunched in the corner, her rasp, "why aren't you outside, because Alvin hits you? that's no reason, go out, scaredy." I knew Emily hated it even if she did not clutch and implore "don't go Mommy" like the other children, mornings.

She always had a reason why we should stay home. Momma, you look sick. Momma, I feel sick. Momma, the teachers aren't there today, they're sick. Momma, we can't go, there was a fire there last night. Momma, it's a holiday today, no school, they told me.

But never a direct protest, never rebellion. I think of our others in their three-, four-year-oldness—the explosions, the tempers, the denunciations, the demands—and I feel suddenly ill. I put the iron down. What in me demanded that goodness in her? And what was the cost, the cost to her of such goodness?

The old man living in the back once said in his gentle way: "You should smile at Emily more when you look at her." What *was* in my face when I looked at her? I loved her. There were all the acts of love.

It was only with the others I remembered what he said, and it was the face of joy, and not of care or tightness or worry I turned to them—too late for Emily. She does not smile easily, let alone almost always as her brothers and sisters do. Her face is closed and sombre, but when she wants, how fluid. You must have seen it in her pantomimes, you spoke of her rare gift for comedy on the stage that rouses a laughter out of the audience so dear they applaud and applaud and do not want to let her go.

Where does it come from, that comedy? There was none of it in

her when she came back to me that second time, after I had had to
send her away again. She had a new daddy now to learn to love, and
I think perhaps it was a better time.

Except when we left her alone nights, telling ourselves she was
old enough.

"Can't you go some other time, Mommy, like tomorrow?" she would
ask. "Will it be just a little while you'll be gone? Do you promise?"

The time we came back, the front door open, the clock on the floor
in the hall. She rigid awake. "It wasn't just a little while. I didn't cry.
Three times I called you, just three times, and then I ran downstairs
to open the door so you could come faster. The clock talked loud. I
threw it away, it scared me what it talked."

She said the clock talked loud again that night I went to the
hospital to have Susan. She was delirious with the fever that comes
before red measles, but she was fully conscious all the week I was
gone and the week after we were home when she could not come
near the new baby or me.

She did not get well. She stayed skeleton thin, not wanting to eat,
and night after night she had nightmares. She would call for me,
and I would rouse from exhaustion to sleepily call back: "You're all
right, darling, go to sleep, it's just a dream," and if she still called,
in a sterner voice, "now go to sleep, Emily, there's nothing to hurt
you." Twice, only twice, when I had to get up for Susan anyhow, I
went in to sit with her.

Now when it is too late (as if she would let me hold and comfort
her like I do the others) I get up and go to her at once at her moan or
restless stirring. "Are you awake, Emily? Can I get you something?"
And the answer is always the same: "No, I'm all right, go back to
sleep, Mother."

They persuaded me at the clinic to send her away to a convales-
cent home in the country where "she can have the kind of food and
care you can't manage for her, and you'll be free to concentrate on
the new baby." They still send children to that place. I see pictures

on the society page of sleek young women planning affairs to raise money for it, or dancing at the affairs, or decorating Easter eggs or filling Christmas stockings for the children.

They never have a picture of the children so I do not know if the girls still wear those gigantic red bows and the ravaged looks on the every other Sunday when parents can come to visit "unless otherwise notified"—as we were notified the first six weeks.

Oh it is a handsome place, green lawns and tall trees and fluted flower beds. High up on the balconies of each cottage the children stand, the girls in their red bows and white dresses, the boys in white suits and giant red ties. The parents stand below shrieking up to be heard and the children shriek down to be heard, and between them the invisible wall "Not To Be Contaminated by Parental Germs or Physical Affection."

There was a tiny girl who always stood hand in hand with Emily. Her parents never came. One visit she was gone. "They moved her to Rose Cottage" Emily shouted in explanation. "They don't like you to love anybody here."

She wrote once a week, the labored writing of a seven-year-old. "I am fine. How is the baby. If I write my leter nicly I will have a star. Love." There never was a star. We wrote every other day, letters she could never hold or keep but only hear read—once. "We simply do not have room for children to keep any personal possessions," they patiently explained when we pieced one Sunday's shrieking together to plead how much it would mean to Emily, who loved so to keep things, to be allowed to keep her letters and cards.

Each visit she looked frailer. "She isn't eating," they told us.

(They had runny eggs for breakfast or mush with lumps, Emily said later, I'd hold it in my mouth and not swallow. Nothing ever tasted good, just when they had chicken.)

It took us eight months to get her released home, and only the fact that she gained back so little of her seven lost pounds convinced the social worker.

9

I used to try to hold and love her after she came back, but her body would stay stiff, and after a while she'd push away. She ate little. Food sickened her, and I think much of life too. Oh she had physical lightness and brightness, twinkling by on skates, bouncing like a ball up and down up and down over the jump rope, skimming over the hill; but these were momentary.

She fretted about her appearance, thin and dark and foreign-looking at a time when every little girl was supposed to look or thought she should look a chubby blonde replica of Shirley Temple. The doorbell sometimes rang for her, but no one seemed to come and play in the house or be a best friend. Maybe because we moved so much.

There was a boy she loved painfully through two school semesters. Months later she told me how she had taken pennies from my purse to buy him candy. "Licorice was his favorite and I brought him some every day, but he still liked Jennifer better'n me. Why, Mommy?" The kind of question for which there is no answer.

School was a worry to her. She was not glib or quick in a world where glibness and quickness were easily confused with ability to learn. To her overworked and exasperated teachers she was an over-conscientious "slow learner" who kept trying to catch up and was absent entirely too often.

I let her be absent, though sometimes the illness was imaginary. How different from my now-strictness about attendance with the others. I wasn't working. We had a new baby, I was home anyhow. Sometimes, after Susan grew old enough, I would keep her home from school, too, to have them all together.

Mostly Emily had asthma, and her breathing, harsh and labored, would fill the house with a curiously tranquil sound. I would bring the two old dresser mirrors and her boxes of collections to her bed. She would select beads and single earrings, bottle tops and shells, dried flowers and pebbles, old postcards and scraps, all sorts of oddments; then she and Susan would play Kingdom, setting up landscapes and furniture, peopling them with action.

Those were the only times of peaceful companionship between her and Susan. I have edged away from it, that poisonous feeling between them, that terrible balancing of hurts and needs I had to do between the two, and did so badly, those earlier years.

Oh there are conflicts between the others too, each one human, needing, demanding, hurting, taking—but only between Emily and Susan, no, Emily toward Susan that corroding resentment. It seems so obvious on the surface, yet it is not obvious. Susan, the second child, Susan, golden- and curly-haired and chubby, quick and articulate and assured, everything in appearance and manner Emily was not; Susan, not able to resist Emily's precious things, losing or sometimes clumsily breaking them; Susan telling jokes and riddles to company for applause while Emily sat silent (to say to me later: that was *my* riddle, Mother, I told it to Susan); Susan, who for all the five years' difference in age was just a year behind Emily in developing physically.

I am glad for that slow physical development that widened the difference between her and her contemporaries, though she suffered over it. She was too vulnerable for that terrible world of youthful competition, of preening and parading, of constant measuring of yourself against every other, of envy, "If I had that copper hair," "If I had that skin. . . ." She tormented herself enough about not looking like the others, there was enough of the unsureness, the having to be conscious of words before you speak, the constant caring—what are they thinking of me? without having it all magnified by the merciless physical drives.

Ronnie is calling. He is wet and I change him. It is rare there is such a cry now. That time of motherhood is almost behind me when the ear is not one's own but must always be racked and listening for the child cry, the child call. We sit for a while and I hold him, looking out over the city spread in charcoal with its soft aisles of light. "*Shoogily*," he breathes and curls closer. I carry him back to bed, asleep. *Shoogily*. A funny word, a family word, inherited from Emily, invented by her to say: *comfort*.

In this and other ways she leaves her seal, I say aloud. And startle at my saying it. What do I mean? What did I start to gather together, to try and make coherent? I was at the terrible, growing years. War years. I do not remember them well. I was working, there were four smaller ones now, there was not time for her. She had to help be a mother, and housekeeper, and shopper. She had to set her seal. Mornings of crisis and near hysteria trying to get lunches packed, hair combed, coats and shoes found, everyone to school or Child Care on time, the baby ready for transportation. And always the paper scribbled on by a smaller one, the book looked at by Susan then mislaid, the homework not done. Running out to that huge school where she was one, she was lost, she was a drop; suffering over her unpreparedness, stammering and unsure in her classes.

There was so little time left at night after the kids were bedded down. She would struggle over books, always eating (it was in those years she developed her enormous appetite that is legendary in our family) and I would be ironing, or preparing food for the next day, or writing V-mail to Bill, or tending the baby. Sometimes, to make me laugh, or out of her despair, she would imitate happenings or types at school.

I think I said once: "Why don't you do something like this in the school amateur show?" One morning she phoned me at work, hardly understandable through the weeping: "Mother, I did it. I won, I won; they gave me first prize; they clapped and clapped and wouldn't let me go."

Now suddenly she was Somebody, and as imprisoned in her difference as she had been in her anonymity.

She began to be asked to perform at other high schools, even in colleges, then at city and statewide affairs. The first one we went to, I only recognized her that first moment when thin, shy, she almost drowned herself into the curtains. Then: Was this Emily? The control, the command, the convulsing and deadly clowning, the spell, then the roaring, stamping audience, unwilling to let this rare and precious laughter out of their lives.

Afterwards: You ought to do something about her with a gift like that—but without money or knowing how, what does one do? We have left it all to her, and the gift has as often eddied inside, clogged and clotted, as been used and growing.

She is coming. She runs up the stairs two at a time with her light graceful step, and I know she is happy tonight. Whatever it was that occasioned your call did not happen today.

"Aren't you ever going to finish the ironing, Mother? Whistler painted his mother in a rocker. I'd have to paint mine standing over an ironing board." This is one of her communicative nights and she tells me everything and nothing as she fixes herself a plate of food out of the icebox.

She is so lovely. Why did you want me to come in at all? Why were you concerned? She will find her way.

She starts up the stairs to bed. "Don't get *me* up with the rest in the morning." "But I thought you were having midterms." "Oh, those," she comes back in, kisses me, and says quite lightly, "in a couple of years when we'll all be atom-dead they won't matter a bit."

She has said it before. She *believes* it. But because I have been dredging the past, and all that compounds a human being is so heavy and meaningful in me, I cannot endure it tonight.

I will never total it all. I will never come in to say: She was a child seldom smiled at. Her father left me before she was a year old. I had to work her first six years when there was work, or I sent her home and to his relatives. There were years she had care she hated. She was dark and thin and foreign-looking in a world where the prestige went to blondeness and curly hair and dimples, she was slow where glibness was prized. She was a child of anxious, not proud, love. We were poor and could not afford for her the soil of easy growth. I was a young mother, I was a distracted mother. There were the other children pushing up, demanding. Her younger sister seemed all that she was not. There were years she did not let me touch her. She kept too much in herself, her life was such she had to keep too much in herself. My wisdom came too late. She has much to her and probably little will come of it. She is a child of her age, of depression, of war, of fear.

Let her be. So all that is in her will not bloom—but in how many does it? There is still enough left to live by. Only help her to know— help make it so there is cause for her to know—that she is more than this dress on the ironing board, helpless before the iron.

1953–1954

HEY SAILOR, WHAT SHIP?

I

The grimy light; the congealing smell of cigarettes that had been smoked long ago and of liquor that had been drunk long ago; the boasting, cursing, wheedling, cringing voices, and the greasy feel of the bar as he gropes for his glass.

Hey Sailor, what ship?

His face flaring in the smoky mirror. The veined gnawing. Wha's it so quiet for? Hey, hit the tune-box. (*Lennie and Helen and the kids.*) Wha time's it anyway? Gotta . . .

Gotta something. Stand watch? No, din't show last night, ain't gonna show tonight, gonna sign off. Out loud: Hell with ship. You got any friends, ship? then hell with your friends. That right Deeck? And he turns to Deeck for approval, but Deeck is gone. Where's Deeck? Givim five bucks and he blows.

All right, says a nameless one, you're loaded. How's about a buck? Less one buck. Company. But he too is gone.

And he digs into his pockets to see how much he has left.

Right breast pocket, a crumpled five. Left pants pocket, three, no, four collapsed one-ers. Left jacket pocket, pawn ticket, Manila; card, "When in Managua it's Marie's for Hospitality"; union book; I.D. stuff; trip card; two ones, one five, accordion-pleated together. Right pants pocket, jingle money. Seventeen bucks. And the hands tremble.

Where'd it all go? and he lurches through the past. One hundred and fifty draw yesterday. No, day before, maybe even day 'fore that. Seven for a bottle when cashed the check, twenty to Blackie, thirty-three back to Goldballs, cab to Frisco, thirty-eight, thirty-nine for the jacket and the kicks (new jacket, new kicks, look good to see Lennie and Helen and the kids), twenty-four smackers dues and ten-dollar fine. That fine. . . .

Hey, to the barkeep, one comin' up. And he swizzles it down, pronto. Twenty and seven and thirty-three and thirty-nine. Ten-dollar fine and five to Frenchy at the hall and drinkin' all night with Johnson, don't know how much, and on the way to the paymaster. . . .

The PAYmaster. Out loud, in angry mimicry, with a slight scandihoovian accent, to nobody, nobody at all: Whaddaya think of that? Hafta be able to sign your name or we can't give you your check. Too stewed to sign your name, he says, no check.

Only seventeen bucks. Hey, to the barkeep, how 'bout advancing me fifty? Hunching over the bar, confidential, so he sees the bottles glistening in the depths. See? and he ruffles in his pockets for the voucher, P.F.E., Michael Jackson, thass me, five hundred and twenty-seven and eleven cents. You don' know me? Been here all night, all day. Bell knows me. Get Bell. Been drinkin' here twenty-three years, every time hit Frisco. Ask Bell.

But Bell sold. Forgot, forgot. Took his cushion and moved to Petaluma to raise chickens. Well hell with you. Got any friends? then hell with your friends. Go to Pearl's. (*Not Lennie and Helen and the kids?*) See what's new, or old. Got 'nuf lettuce for *them* babies.

But the idea is visual, not physical. Get a bottle first. And he waits for the feeling good that should be there, but there is none, only a sickness lurking.

The Bulkhead sign bile green in the rain. Rain and the street clogged with cars, going-home-from-work cars. Screw 'em all. He starts across. Screech, screech, screech. Brakes jammed on for a block back. M. Norbert Jacklebaum makes 'em stop; said without glee. On to Pearl's. But someone is calling. Whitey, Whitey, get in here you stumblebum. And it is Lennie, a worn likeness of Lennie, so changed he gets in all right, but does not ask questions or answer them. (Are you on a ship or on the beach? How long was the trip? You sick, man, or just stewed? Only three or four days and you're feeling like this? *No*, no stopping for a bottle or to buy presents.)

He only sits while the sickness crouches underneath, waiting to spring, and it muddles in his head, *going to see Lennie and Helen and the kids, no presents for 'em, an' don't even feel good.*

Hey Sailor, what ship?

2

And so he gets there after all, four days and everything else too late. It is an old peaked house on a hill and he has imaged and entered it over and over again, in a thousand various places a thousand various times: on watch and over chow, lying on his bunk or breezing with the guys; from sidewalk beds and doorway shelters, in flophouses and jails; sitting silent at union meetings or waiting in the places one waits, or listening to the Come to Jesus boys.

The stairs are innumerable and he barely makes it to the top. Helen (Helen? so . . . grayed?), Carol, Allie, surging upon him. A fever of hugging and kissing. 'Sabout time, shrills Carol over and over again. 'Sabout time.

Who is real and who is not? Jeannie, taller than Helen suddenly, just standing there, watching. I'm in first grade now, yells Allie, now you can fix my dolly crib, Whitey, it's smashted.

You hit it just right. We've got stew, pressure cooker stuff, but your favorite anyway. How long since you've eaten? And Helen looks at him, kisses him again, and begins to cry.

Mother! orders Jeannie, and marches her into the kitchen.

Whassmatter Helen? One look at me, she begins to cry.

She's glad to see you, you S.O.B.

Whassmatter her? She don't look so good.

You don't look so good either, Lennie says grimly. Better sit for a while.

Mommy oughta quit work, volunteers Carol; she's tired. All the time.

Whirl me round like you always do, Whitey, whirl me round, begs Allie.

Where did you go this time, Whitey? asks Carol. Thought you were going to send me stamps for my collection. Why didn't you come Christmas? Can you help me make a puppet stage?

Cut it, kids, not so many questions, orders Lennie, going up the stairs to wash. Whitey's got to take it easy. We'll hear about everything after dinner.

Your shoes are shiny, says Allie. Becky in my class got new shoes too, Mary Janes, but they're fuzzy. And she kneels down to pat his shoes.

Forgotten, how big the living room was. (And is he really here?) Carol reads the funnies on the floor, her can up in the air. Allie inspects him gravely. You got a new hurt on your face, Whitey. Sing a song, or say Thou Crown 'n Deep. And after dinner can I bounce on you?

Not so many questions, repeats Carol.

Whitey's just gonna sit here. . . . Should go in the kitchen. Help your mommy.

Angry from the kitchen: Well, I don't care. I'm calling Marilyn

and tell her not to come; we'll do our homework over there. I'm
certainly not going to take a chance and let her come over here.

Shhh, Jeannie, shhh. He beg that, or Helen? The windows are
blind with steam, all hidden behind them the city, the bay, the ships.
And is it chow time already? He starts up to go, but it seems he
lurched and fell, for the sickness springs at last and consumes him.
And now Allie is sitting with him. C'mon, sit up and eat, Whitey,
Mommy says you have to eat; I'll eat too. Perched beside him, pretty
as you please. I'll take a forkful and you take a forkful. You're sloppy,
Whitey—for it trickles down his chin. It does not taste; the inside of
him burns. She chatters and then the plate is gone and now the city
sparkles at him through the windows. Helen and Lennie are sitting
there and somebody who looks like somebody he knows.

Chris, reminds Lennie. Don't you remember Chris, the grocery
boy when we lived on Aerial way? We told you he's a M.D. now. Fat
and a poppa and smug; aren't you smug, Chris?

I almost shipped with you once, Whitey. Don't you remember?

(Long ago. Oh yes, oh yes, but there was no permit to be had; and
even if there had been, by that time I didn't have no drag.) Aloud:
I remember. You still got the itch? That's why you came round, to
get fixed up with a trip card?

I came around to look at you. But that was all he was doing, just
sitting there and looking.

Whassmatter? Don't like my looks? Get too beautiful since you
last saw me? Handsome new nose 'n everything.

You got too beautiful. Where can I take him, Helen?

Can't take me no place. M. Norbert Jacklebaum's fine.

You've got to get up anyhow, Whitey, so I can make up the couch.
Go on, go upstairs with Chris. You're in luck, I even found a clean
sheet.

He settles back down on the couch, the lean scarred arms bent under
his head for a pillow, the muscles ridged like rope.

He's a lousy doc. Affectionately. Gives me a shot of B-1, sleeping pills, and some bum advice. . . . Whaddaya think of that, he remembered me. Thirteen years and he remembers me.

How could he help remembering you with all the hell his father used to raise cause he'd forget his deliveries listening to your lousy stories? You were his he-ro. . . . How do you like the fire?

Your wood, Whitey, says Helen. Still the stuff you chopped three years back. Needs restacking though.

Get right up and do it. . . . Whadja call him for?

You scared us. Don't forget, your last trip up here was for five weeks in Marine Hospital.

We never saw it hit you like this before, says Lennie. After a five-, six-week tear maybe, but you say this was a couple days. You were really out.

Just catching up on my sleep, tha's all.

There is a new picture over the lamp. Bleached hills, a fresh-ploughed field, red horses and a blue-overalled figure.

I got a draw coming. More'n five hundred. How's financial situation round here?

We're eating.

Allie say she want me to fix something? Or was it Carol? Those kids are sure. . . . A year'n a half. . . . An effort to talk, for the sleeping pills are already gripping him, and the languid fire, and the rain that has started up again and cannot pierce the windows. How *you* feeling, Helen? She looks more like Helen now.

Keeping my head above water. She would tell him later. She always told him later, when he would be helping in the kitchen maybe, and suddenly it would come out, how she really was and what was really happening, sometimes things she wouldn't even tell Lennie. And this time, the way she looked, the way Lennie looked. . . .

Allie is on the stairs: I had a bad dream, Mommy. Let me stay here till Jeannie comes to bed with me, Mommy. By Whitey.

What was your bad dream, sweetheart?

Lovingly she puts her arms around his neck, curls up. I was losted, she whispers, and instantly is asleep.

He starts as if he has been burned, and quick lest he wake her, begins stroking her soft hair. It is destroying, dissolving him utterly, this helpless warmth against him, this feel of a child—lost country to him and unattainable.

Sure were a lot of kids begging, he says aloud. I think it's worse.

Korea? asks Len.

Never got ashore in Korea. Yokohama, Cebu, Manila. (The begging children and the lost, the thieving children and the children who were sold.) And he strokes, strokes Allie's soft hair as if the strokes would solidify, dense into a protection.

We lay around Pusan six weeks. Forty-three days on that tub no bigger'n this house and they wouldn't give us no leave ashore. Forty-three days. Len, I never had a drop, you believe me, Len?

Felt good most of this trip, Len, just glad to be sailing again, after Pedro. Always a argument. Somebody says, Christ it's cold, colder'n a whore's heart, and somebody jumps right in and says, colder'n a whore's heart, hell, you ever in Kobe and broke and Kumi didn't give you five yen? And then it starts. Both sides.

Len and Helen like those stories. Tell another. Effort.

You should hear this Stover. Ask him, was you ever in England? and he claps his hands to his head and says, was I ever in England, Oh boy, was I ever in England, those limeys, they beat you with bottles. Ask him, was you ever in Marseilles and he claps his hands to his head and says, was I ever in Marseilles, Oh boy, was I ever in Marseilles, them frogs, they kick you with spikes in their shoes. Ask him, was you ever in Shanghai, and he says, was I ever in Shanghai, was I ever in Shanghai, man, they throw the crockery and the stools at you. Thass everyplace you mention, a different kind of beating.

There was this kid on board, Howie Adams. Gotta bring him up here. Told him 'bout you. Best people in the world, I says, always open house. Best kid. Not like those scenery bums and cherry pickers we got sailing nowadays. Guess what, they made me ship's delegate.

Well, why not? asks Helen; you were probably the best man on board.

A tide of peaceful drowsiness washes over the tumult in him; he is almost asleep, though the veined brown hand still tremblingly strokes, strokes Allie's soft pale hair.

Is that Helen? No, it is Jeannie, so much like Helen of years ago, suddenly there under the hall light, looking in at them all, her cheeks glistening from the rain.

Never saw so many peaceful wrecks in my life. Her look is loving. That's what I want to be when I grow up, just a peaceful wreck holding hands with other peaceful wrecks (For Len and Helen are holding hands). We really fixed Mr. Nickerson. Marilyn did my English, I did her algebra, and her brother Tommy, wrote for us "I will not" five hundred times; then we just tagged on "talk in class, talk in class, talk in class."

She drops her books, kneels down beside Whitey, and using his long ago greeting asks softly, Hey Sailor, what ship?, then turns to her parents. Study in contrasts, Allie's face and Whitey's, where's my camera? Did you tell Whitey I'm graduating in three weeks, do you think you'll be here then, Whitey, and be . . . all right? I'll give you my diploma and write in your name so you can pretend you got though junior high, too. Allie's sure glad you came.

And without warning, with a touch so light, so faint, it seems to breathe against his cheek, she traces a scar. That's a new one, isn't it? Allie noticed. She asked me, does it hurt? Does it?

He stops stroking Allie's hair a moment, starts up again desperately, looks so ill, Helen says sharply: It's late. Better go to bed, Jeannie, there's school tomorrow.

It's late, it's early. Kissing him, Helen, Lennie. Good night. Shall I take my stinky little sister upstairs to bed with me whatever she's doing down here, or shall I leave her for one of you strong men to carry?

Leaning from the middle stair: didn't know you were sick, Whitey, thought you were like . . . some of the other times. From the top stair: see you later, alligators.

Most he wants alone now, alone and a drink, perhaps sleep. And they know. We're going to bed now too. Six comes awful early.

So he endures Helen's kiss too, and Len's affectionate poke. And as Len carries Allie up the stairs, the fire leaps up, kindles Len's shadow so that it seems a dozen bent men cradle a child up endless stairs, while the rain traces on the windows, beseechingly, ceaselessly, like seeking fingers of the blind.

Hey Sailor, what ship? Hey Sailor, what ship?

3

In his sleep he speaks often and loudly, sometimes moans, and toward morning begins the trembling. He wakes into an unshared silence he does not recognize, accustomed so to the various voices of the sea, the multi-pitch of those with whom sleep as well as work and food is shared, the throb of engines, churn of the propeller; or hazed through drink, the noises of the street, or the thin walls like ears—magnifying into lives as senseless as one's own.

Here there is only the whisper of the clock (motor by which this house runs now) and the sounds of oneself.

The trembling will not cease. In the kitchen there is a note:

Bacon and eggs in the icebox and coffee's made. The kids are com-ing straight home from school to be with you. DON'T go down to the front, Lennie'll take you tomorrow. Love.

Love.

The row of cans on the cupboard shelves is thin. So things are still bad, he thinks, no money for stocking up. He opens all the doors hopefully, but if there is a bottle, it is hidden. A long time he stares at the floor, goes out into the yard where fallen rain beads the grasses that will be weeds soon enough, comes back, stares at his dampened feet, stares at the floor some more (needs scrubbing, and the woodwork can stand some too; well, maybe after I feel better), but there are no dishes in the sink, it is all cleaner than he expected.

Upstairs, incredibly, the beds are made, no clothes crumpled on the floor. Except in Jeannie's and Allie's room: there, as remembered, the dust feathers in the corners and dolls sprawl with books, records, and underwear. Guess she'll never get it clean. And up rises his old vision, of how he will return here, laden with groceries, no one in the littered house, and quickly, before they come, straighten the upstairs (the grime in the washbasin), clean the downstairs, scrub the kitchen floor, wash the hills of dishes, put potatoes in and light the oven, and when they finally troop in say, calmly, Helen, the house is clean, and there's steak for dinner.

Whether it is this that hurts in his stomach or the burning chill that will not stop, he dresses himself hastily, arguing with the new shoes that glint with a life all their own. On his way out, he stops for a minute to gloss his hand over the bookcase. Damn good paint job, he says out loud, if I say so myself. Still stands up after fourteen years. Real good that red backing Helen liked so much 'cause it shows above the books.

Hey Sailor, what ship?

4

It is five days before he comes again. A cabbie precedes him up the stairs, loaded with bundles. Right through, right into the kitchen, man, directs Whitey, feeling good, oh quite obviously feeling good. The shoes are spotted now, he wears a torn Melton in place of the new jacket. Groceries, he announces heavily, indicating the packages plopped down. Steak. Whatever you're eating, throw it out.

Didn't I tell you they're a good-looking bunch? triumphantly indicating around the table. 'Cept that Lennie hyena over there. Go on, man, take the whole five smackers.

Don't let him go, Whitey, I wanta ride in the cab, screams Allie.

To the top of the next hill and back, it's a winding curly round and round road, yells Carol.

I'll go too, says Jeannie.

Shut up, Lennie explodes, let the man go, he's working. Sit down, kids. Sit down, Whitey.

Set another plate, Jeannie, says Helen.

An' bring glasses. Got coke for the kids. We gonna have a drink.

I want a cab ride, Allie insists.

Wait till your mean old bastard father's not lookin'. Then we'll go.

Watch the language, Whitey, there's a gentleman present, says Helen. Finish your plate, Allie.

Thass right. Know who the gen'lmun is? I'm the gen'lmun. The world, says Marx, is divided into two classes. . . .

Seafaring gen'lmun and shoreside bastards, choruses Lennie with him.

Why, Daddy! says Jeannie.

You're a mean ole bassard father, says Allie.

Thass right, tell him off, urges Whitey. Hell with waitin' for glasses. Down the ol' hatch.

My class is divided by marks, says Carol, giggling helplessly at her own joke, and anyway what about ladies? Where's *my* drink? Down the hatch.

I got presents, kids. In the kitchen.

Where they'll stay, warns Helen, till after dinner. Just keep sitting.

Course Jeannie over there doesn't care 'bout a present. She's too grown up. Royal highness doesn't even kiss old Whitey, just slams a plate at him.

Fork, knife, spoon too, says Jeannie, why don't you use them?

Good chow, Helen. But he hardly eats, and as they clear the table, he lays down a tenner.

All right, sailor, says Lennie, put your money back.

I'll take it, says Carol, if it's an orphan.

If you get into the front room quick, says Lennie, you won't have to do the dishes.

Who gives a shit about the dishes?

Watch it, says Helen.

Whenja start doin' dishes in this house after dinner anyway?

Since we got organized, says Lennie, always get things done when they're supposed to be. Organized the life out of ourselves. That's what's the matter with Helen.

Well, when you work, Helen starts to explain.

Lookit Daddy kiss Mommy.

Give me my present and whirl me, Whitey, whirl me, demands Allie.

No whirling. Jus' sat down, honey. How'd it be if I bounce you? Lef' my ol' lady in New Orleans with twenny-four kids and a can of beans.

Guess you think 'cause I'm ten I'm too big to bounce any more, says Carol.

Bounce everybody. Jeannie. Your mom. Even Lennie.

What is life
Without a wife (bounce)
And a home (bounce bounce)
Without a baby?

Hey, Helen, bring in those presents. Tell Jeannie, don't come in here, don't get a present. Jeannie, play those marimba records. Want marimba. Feel good, sure feel good. Hey, Lennie, get your wild ass in here, got things to tell you. Leave the women do the work.

Wild ass, giggles Allie.

Jeannie gets mad when you talk like that, says Carol. Give us our presents and let's have a cab ride and tell us about the time you were torpedoed.

Tell us Crown 'n Deep.

Go tell yourself. I'm gonner have a drink.

Down the hatch, Whitey.

Down the hatch.

Better taper off, guy, says Lennie, coming in. We want to have an evening.

Tell Helen bring the presents. She don't hafta be jealous. I got money for her. Helen likes money.

Upstairs, says Helen, they'll get their presents upstairs. After they're ready for bed. There's school tomorrow.

First we'll get them after dinner and now after we're ready for bed. That's not fair, wails Allie.

I never showed him my album yet, says Carol. He never said Crown n' Deep yet.

It isn't fair. We never had our cab ride.

Whitey'll be here tomorrow, says Helen.

Maybe he won't, says Carol. He's got a room rented, he told me. Six weeks' rent in advance and furnished with eighteen cans of beans and thirty-six cans of sardines. All shored up, says Whitey. Somebody called Deeck stays there too.

Lef' my wile ass in New Orleans, twenty-four kids and a present of beans, chants Allie, bouncing herself up and down on the couch. And it's not *fair*.

Say good night to them, Whitey, they'll come down in their night-gowns for a good-night kiss later.

Go on, kids. Mind your momma, don't be like me. An' here's a dollar for you an' a dollar for you. An' a drink for me.

But Lennie has taken the bottle. Whass matter, doncha like to see me feelin' good? Well, screw you, brother, I'm supplied, and he pulls a pint out of his pocket.

Listen, Whitey, says Jeannie, I've got some friends coming over and . . . Whitey, please, they're not used to your kind of language.

That so? 'Scuse me, your royal highness. Here's ten dollars, your royal highness. Help you forgive?

Please go sit in the kitchen. Please, Daddy, take him in the kitchen with you.

Jeannie, says Lennie, give him back the money.

He gave it to me, it's mine.

Give it back.

All right. Flinging it down, running up the stairs.

Quit it, Whitey, says Lennie.

Quit what?

Throwing your goddam money around. Where do you think you are, down on the front?

'S better down on the front. You're gettin' holier than the dago pope.

I mean it, guy. And tone down that language. Let's have the bottle.

No. Into the pocket. Do *you* good to feel good for a change. You 'n Helen look like you been through the meat grinder.

Silence.

Gently: Tell me about the trip, Whitey.

Good trip. Most of the time. 'Lected me ship's delegate.

You told us.

Tell you 'bout that kid, Howie? Best kid. Got my gear off the ship and lef' it down at the hall for me. Whaddaya think of that?

(Oh feeling good, come back, come back.)

Jeannie in her hat and coat. Stiffly. Thank you for the earrings, Whitey.

Real crystals. Best . . . Lennie, 'm gonna give her ten dollars. For treat her friends. After all, ain't she my wife?

Whitey, do I have to hear that story again? I was four years old.

Again? (He had told the story so often, as often as anyone would listen, whenever he felt good, and always as he told it, the same shy

28

happiness would wing through him, how when she was four, she had crawled into bed beside him one morning, announcing triumphantly to her mother: I'm married to Whitey now, I don't have to sleep by myself any more.) Sorry, royal highness, won't mention it. How's watch I gave you, remember?

(Not what he means to say at all. Remember the love I gave you, the worship offered, the toys I mended and made, the questions answered, the care for you, the pride in you.)

I lost the watch, remember? 'I was too young for such expensive presents.' You keep talking about it because that's the only reason you give presents, to buy people to be nice to you and to yak about the presents when you're drunk. Here's your earrings too. I'm going outside to wait for my friends.

Jeannie! It is Helen, back down with the kids. Jeannie, come into the kitchen with me.

Jeannie's gonna get heck, says Carol. Geeeee, down the hatch. Wish *I* could swallow so long. Is my dresser set solid gold like it looks?

Kiss the dolly you gave me, says Allie. She's your grandchild now. You kiss her too, Daddy. I bet she was the biggest dolly in the store.

Your dolly can't talk. Thass good, honey, that she can't talk.

Here's my album, Whitey. It's got a picture of you. Is that really you, Whitey? It don't look like. . . .

Don't look, he says to himself, closing his eyes. Don't look. But it is indelible. Under the joyful sun, proud sea, proud ship as background, the proud young man, glistening hair and eyes, joyful body, face open to life, unlined. Sixteen? Seventeen? Close it up, he says, M. Norbert Jacklebaum never saw the guy. Quit punchin' me.

Nobody's punchin' you Whitey, says Allie. You're feeling your face.

Tracing the scars, the pits and lines, the battered nose; seeking to find.

Your name's Michael Jackson, Whitey, why do you always say Jacklebaum? marvels Allie.

Tell Crown 'n Deep. I try to remember it and I never can, Carol says, softly. Neither can Jeannie. Tell Crown 'n Deep, tell how you learnt it. If you feel like. Please.

Oh yes, he feels like. *When there is November in my soul,* he begins. No, wrong one.

Taking the old proud stance. The Valedictory, written the dawn 'fore he was executed by Jose Rizal, national hero of the Philippines. Taught me by Li'l Joe Roco, not much taller'n you, Jeannie, my first shipmate.

I'm Carol, not Jeannie.

Li'l Joe. Never got back home, they were puttin' the hatch covers on and . . . I only say it when it's special. Jose Rizal: El Ultimo Adiós. Known as The Valedictory, 1896.

Land I adore, farewell. . . .
Our forfeited garden of Eden,
Joyous I yield up for thee my sad life
And were it far brighter,
Young or rose-strewn, still would I give it.

Vision I followed from afar,
Desire that spurred on and consumed me,
Beautiful it is to fall,
That the vision may rise to fulfillment.

Go on, Whitey.

Little will matter, my country,
That thou shouldst forget me.
I shall be speech in thy ears, fragrance and color,
Light and shout and loved song. . . .

Inaudible.

O crown and deep of my sorrows,
I am leaving all with thee, my friends, my love,
Where I go are no tyrants. . . .

He stands there, swaying. Say good night, says Lennie. Whitey'll tell it all some other time. . . . Here, guy, sit down.

And in the kitchen.

You know how he talks. How can you let him? In front of the little kids.

They don't hear the words, they hear what's behind them. There are worse words than cuss words, there are words that hurt. When Whitey talks like that, it's everyday words; the men he lives with talk like that, that's all.

Well, not the kind of men I want to know. I don't go over to anybody's house and hear words like that.

Jeannie, who are you kidding? You kids use them all.

That's different, that's being grown-up, like smoking. And he's so drunk. Why didn't Daddy let me keep the ten dollars? It would mean a lot to me, and it doesn't mean anything to him.

It's his money. He worked for it, it's the only power he has. We don't take Whitey's money.

Oh no. Except when he gives it to you.

When he was staying with us, when they were rocking chair, unemployment checks, it was different. He was sober. It was his share.

He's just a Howard Street wino now—why don't you and Daddy kick him out of the house? He doesn't belong here.

Of course he belongs here, he's a part of us, like family. . . . Jeannie, this is the only house in the world he can come into and be around people without having to pay.

Somebody who brings presents and whirls you around and expects you to jump for his old money.

Remember how good he's been to you. To us. Jeannie, he was only a few years older than you when he started going to sea.

Now you're going to tell me the one about how he saved Daddy's life in the strike in 1934.

31

He knows more about people and places than almost anyone I've ever known. You can learn from him.

When's he like that any more? He's just a Howard Street wino, that's all.

Jeannie, I care you should understand. You think Mr. Norris is a tragedy, you feel sorry for him because he talks intelligent and lives in a nice house and has quiet drunks. You've got to understand.

Just a wino. Even if it's whisky when he's got the money. Which isn't for long.

To understand.

In the beginning there had been youth and the joy of raising hell and that curious inability to take a whore unless he were high with drink.

And later there were memories to forget, dreams to be stifled, hopes to be murdered.

Know who was the ol' man on the ship? Blackie Karns, Kissass Karns hisself.

Started right when you did, Whitey.

Oh yes. (A few had nimbly, limberly clambered up.) Remember in the war he was the only one of us would wear his braid uptown? That one year I made mate? Know how to deal with you, Jackson, he says. No place for you on the ships any more, he says. My asshole still knows more than all of you put together, I says.

What was it all about, Whitey?

Don' remember. Rotten feed. Bring him up a plate and say, eat it yourself. Nobody gonna do much till we get better. We got better.

This kid, overtime comin' to him. Didn't even wanta beef about it. I did it anyway. Got fined by the union for takin' it up. M. Norbert Jacklebaum fined by the union, "conduct unbefitting ship's delegate" says the Patrolman, "not taking it up through proper channels." (His old fine talent for mimicry jutting through the blurred-together words.)

These kids, these cherry pickers, they don't realize how we got what we got. Beginnin' to lose it, too. Think anybody backed me up, Len? Just this Howie and a scenery bum, Goldballs, gonna write a book. Have you in it, Jackson, he says, you're a real salt.

Understand. The death of the brotherhood. Once, once an injury to one is an injury to all. Once, once they had to live for each other. And whoever came off the ship fat shared, because that was the only way of survival for all of them, the easy sharing, the knowing that when you needed, waiting for a trip card to come up, you'd be staked.

Now it was a dwindling few, and more and more of them winos, who shipped sometimes or had long ago irrevocably lost their book for nonpayment of dues.

Hey, came here to feel good. Down the hatch. Hell with you. You got any friends? Hell with your friends.

Helen is back. So you still remember El Ultimo, Whitey. Remember when we first heard Joe recite it?

I remember.

Remember too much, too goddam much. For twenty-three years, the watery shifting: many faces, many places.

But more and more, certain things the same. The gin mills and the cathouses. The calabozas and jails and stockades. More and more New York and Norfolk and New Orleans and Pedro and Frisco and Seattle like the foreign ports: docks, clip joints, hockshops, cathouses, skid rows, the Law and the Wall: only so far shall you go and no further, uptown forbidden, not your language, not your people, not your country.

Added sometimes now, the hospital.

What's going to happen with you, Whitey?

What I care? Nobody hasta care what happens to M. Jacklebaum.

How can we help caring, Whitey? Jesus, man, you're a chunk of our lives.

Shove it, Lennie. So you're a chunk of my life. So?

Understand. Once they had been young together.

To Lennie he remained a tie to adventure and a world in which men had not eaten each other; and the pleasure, when the mind was clear, of chewing over with that tough mind the happenings of the times or the queernesses of people, or laughing over the mimicry.

To Helen he was the compound of much help given, much support: the ear to hear, the hand that understands how much a scrubbed floor, or a washed dish, or a child taken care of for a while, can mean.

They had believed in his salvation, once. Get him away from the front where he has to drink for company and for a woman. The torn-out-of-him confession, the drunken end of his eight-months-sober try to make a go of it on the beach—don't you see, I can't go near a whore unless I'm lit?

If they could know what it is like now, so casual as if it were after thirty years of marriage.

Later, the times he had left money with them for plans: fix his teeth, buy a car, get into the Ship Painters, go see his family in Chi. But soon enough the demands for the money when the drunken need was on him, so that after a few tries they gave up trying to keep it for him.

Later still, the first time it became too much and Lennie forbade the house to him unless he were "O.K."—"because of the children."

Now the decaying body, the body that was betraying him. And the memories to forget, the dreams to be stifled, the hopeless hopes to be murdered.

What's going to happen with you, Whitey? Helen repeats. I never know if you'll be back. If you'll be able to be back.

He tips the bottle to the end. Thirstily he thinks: Deeck and his room where he can yell or sing or pound and Deeck will look on without reproach or pity or anguish.

I'm goin' now.

Wait, Whitey. We'll drive you. Want to know where you're shacked, anyway.

Go own steam. Send you a card.

By Jeannie, silent and shrunken into her coat. He passes no one in the streets. They are inside, each in his slab of house, watching the flickering light of television. The sullen fog is on his face, but by the time he has walked to the third hill, it has lifted so he can see the city below him, wave after wave, and there at the crest, the tiny house he has left, its eyes unshaded. After a while they blur with the myriad others that stare at him so blindly.

Then he goes down.

Hey Sailor, what ship?
Hey Marinero, what ship?

San Francisco 1953–1955

For Jack Eggan, Seaman 1915–1938
Killed in the retreat across the Ebro, Spain

O YES

I

They are the only white people there, sitting in the dimness of the Negro church that had once been a corner store, and all through the bubbling, swelling, seething of before the services, twelve-year-old Carol clenches tight her mother's hand, the other resting lightly on her friend, Parialee Phillips, for whose baptism she has come.

The white-gloved ushers hurry up and down the aisle, beckoning people to their seats. A jostle of people. To the chairs angled to the left for the youth choir, to the chairs angled to the right for the ladies' choir, even up to the platform, where behind the place for the dignitaries and mixed choir, the new baptismal tank gleams—and as if pouring into it from the ceiling, the blue-painted River of Jordan, God standing in the waters, embracing a brown man in a leopard skin and pointing to the letters of gold:

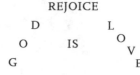

REJOICE

                D   L
          O   IS   O
                                              V
          G   E

I AM THE WAY   THE TRUTH   THE LIFE

At the clear window, the crucified Christ embroidered on the starched white curtain leaps in the wind of the sudden singing. And the choirs march in. Robes of wine, of blue, of red.

"We stands and sings too," says Parialee's mother, Alva, to Helen; though already Parialee has pulled Carol up. Singing, little Lucinda Phillips fluffs out her many petticoats; singing, little Bubbie bounces up and down on his heels.

Any day now I'll reach that land of freedom,
                                                    Yes, o yes
Any day now, know that promised land

The youth choir claps and taps to accent the swing of it. Beginning to tap, Carol stiffens. "Parry, look. Somebody from school."

"Once more once," says Parialee, in the new way she likes to talk now.

"Eddie Garlin's up there. He's in my math."

"Couple cats from Franklin Jr. chirps in the choir. No harm or alarm."

Anxiously Carol scans the faces to see who else she might know, who else might know her, but looks quickly down to Lucinda's wide skirts, for it seems Eddie looks back at her, sullen or troubled, though it is hard to tell, faced as she is into the window of curtained sunblaze.

I know my robe will fit me well
I tried it on at the gates of hell

If it were a record she would play it over and over, Carol thought, to untwine the intertwined voices, to search how the many rhythms rock apart and yet are one glad rhythm.

When I get to heaven gonna sing and shout
Nobody be able to turn me out

"That's Mr. Chairback Evans going to invocate," Lucinda leans across Parry to explain. "He don't invoke good like Momma."

"Shhhh."

"Momma's the only lady in the church that invocates. She made the prayer last week. (Last month, Lucy.) I made the children's 'nouncement last time. (That was way back Thanksgiving.) And Bubbie's 'nounced too. Lots of times."

"Lucy-inda. SIT!"

Bible study announcements and mixed-choir practice announcements and Teen Age Hearts meeting announcements.

If Eddie said something to her about being there, worried Carol, if he talked to her right in front of somebody at school.

Messengers of Faith announcements and Mamboettes announcement and Committee for the Musical Tea.

Parry's arm so warm. Not realizing, starting up the old game from grade school, drumming a rhythm on the other's arm to see if the song could be guessed. "Parry, guess."

But Parry is pondering the platform.

The baptismal tank? "Parry, are you scared . . . the baptizing?"

"This cat? No." Shaking her head so slow and scornful, the barrette in her hair, sun fired, strikes a long rail of light. And still ponders the platform.

New Strangers Baptist Church invites you and Canaan Fair Singers announcements and Battle of Song and Cosmopolites meet. "O Lord, I couldn't find no ease," a solo. The ladies' choir:

O what you say seekers, o what you say seekers,
Will you never turn back no more?

The mixed choir sings:

Ezekiel saw that wheel of time
Every spoke was of humankind . . .

And the slim worn man in the pin-stripe suit starts his sermon
On the Nature of God. How God is long-suffering. Oh, how long
he has suffered. Calling the roll of the mighty nations, that rose and
fell and now are dust for grinding the face of Man.

O voice of drowsiness and dream to which Carol does not need to
listen. As long ago. Parry warm beside her too, as it used to be, there
in the classroom at Mann Elementary, and the feel of drenched in
sun and dimness and dream. Smell and sound of the chalk wearing
itself away to nothing, rustle of books, drumming tattoo of Parry's
fingers on her arm: *Guess.*

And as the preacher's voice spins happy and free, it is the used-
to-be play-yard. Tag. Thump of the volley ball. Ecstasy of the jump
rope. Parry, do pepper. Carol, do pepper. Parry's bettern Carol, Carol's
bettern Parry. . . .

Did someone scream?

It seemed someone screamed—but all were sitting as before,
though the sun no longer blared through the windows. She tried to
see up where Eddie was, but the ushers were standing at the head
of the aisle now, the ladies in white dresses like nurses or waitresses
wear, the men holding their white-gloved hands up so one could see
their palms.

"And God is Powerful," the preacher was chanting. "Nothing for
him to scoop out the oceans and pat up the mountains. Nothing for
him to scoop up the miry clay and create man. Man, I said, create Man."

The lady in front of her moaned "*O yes*" and others were moaning
"*O yes.*"

"And when the earth mourned the Lord said, Weep not, for all
will be returned to you, every dust, every atom. And the tired dust
settles back, goes back. Until that Judgment Day. That great day."

"*O yes.*"

The ushers were giving out fans. Carol reached for one and Parry said: "What *you* need one for?" but she took it anyway.

"You think Satchmo can blow; you think Muggsy can blow; you think Dizzy can blow?" He was straining to an imaginary trumpet now, his head far back and his voice coming out like a trumpet.

"Oh Parry, he's so good."

"Well. Jelly jelly."

"Nothing to Gabriel on that great getting-up morning. And the horn wakes up Adam, and Adam runs to wake up Eve, and Eve moans; Just one more minute, let me sleep, and Adam yells, Great Day, woman, don't you know it's the Great Day?"

"*Great Day, Great Day*," the mixed choir behind the preacher rejoices:

When our cares are past
when we're home at last . . .

"And Eve runs to wake up Cain." Running round the platform, stooping and shaking imaginary sleepers, "and Cain runs to wake up Abel." Looping, scalloping his voice—"Grea-aaa-aat Daaaay." All the choirs thundering:

Great Day
When the battle's fought
And the victory's won

Exultant spirals of sound. And Carol caught into it (Eddie forgotten, the game forgotten) chanting with Lucy and Bubbie: "*Great Day.*"

"Ohhhhhhhhhh," his voice like a trumpet again, "the re-unioning. Ohhhhhhhhh, the rejoicing. After the ages immemorial of longing."

Someone *was* screaming. And an awful thrumming sound with it, like feet and hands thrashing around, like a giant jumping of a rope.

"*Great Day.*" And no one stirred or stared as the ushers brought a little woman out into the aisle, screaming and shaking, just a little shrunk-up woman, not much taller than Carol, the biggest thing about her her swollen hands and the cascades of tears wearing her face.

The shaking inside Carol too. Turning and trembling to ask: "What . . . that lady?" But Parry still ponders the platform; little Lucy loops the chain of her bracelet round and round; and Bubbie sits placidly, dreamily. Alva Phillips is up fanning a lady in front of her; two lady ushers are fanning other people Carol cannot see. And her mother, her mother looks in a sleep.

Yes. He raised up the dead from the grave. He made old death behave.

Yes. Yes. From all over, hushed.   *O Yes*
He was your mother's rock. Your father's mighty tower. And he gave us a little baby. A little baby to love.

I am so glad
Yes, your friend, when you're friendless. Your father when you're fatherless. Way maker. Door opener.

Yes
When it seems you can't go on any longer, he's there. You can, he says, you can.

Yes
And that burden you been carrying—ohhhhh that burden—not for always will it be. No, not for always.

Stay with me, Lord
I will put my Word in you and it is power. I will put my Truth in you and it is power.

O Yes
Out of your suffering I will make you to stand as a stone. A tried stone. Hewn out of the mountains of ages eternal.
Ohhhhhhhhhhh. Out of the mire I will lift your feet. Your tired feet from so much wandering. From so much work and wear and hard times.

Yes

From so much journeying—and never the promised land. And I'll wash them in the well your tears made. And I'll shod them in the gospel of peace, and of feeling good. Ohhhhhhhhh.

O Yes.

Behind Carol, a trembling wavering scream. Then the thrashing. Up above, the singing:

They taken my blessed Jesus and flogged him to the woods
And they made him hew out his cross and they dragged him to Calvary
Shout brother, Shout shout shout. He never cried a word.

Powerful throbbing voices. Calling and answering to each other.

They taken my blessed Jesus and whipped him up the hill
With a knotty whip and a raggedy thorn he never cried a word
Shout, sister. Shout shout shout. He never cried a word.
Go tell the people the Saviour has risen
Has risen from the dead and will live forevermore
   And won't have to die no more.
Halleloo.
  Shout, brother, shout
  We won't have to die no more!

A single exultant lunge of shriek. Then the thrashing. All around a clapping. Shouts with it. The piano whipping, whipping air to a froth. Singing now.

I once was lost who now am found
Was blind who now can see

On Carol's fan, a little Jesus walked on wondrously blue waters to where bearded disciples spread nets out of a fishing boat. If she studied the fan—became it—it might make a wall around her. If she could make what was happening (*what* was happening?) into a record small and round to listen to far and far as if into a seashell—the stamp and rills and spirals all tiny (but never any screaming).

wade wade in the water

Jordan's water is chilly and wild
I've got to get home to the other side
God's going to trouble the waters

The music leaps and prowls. Ladders of screamings. Drumming feet of ushers running. And still little Lucy fluffs her skirts, loops the chain on her bracelet; still Bubbie sits and rocks dreamily; and only eyes turn for an instant to the aisle as if nothing were happening. "Mother, let's go home," Carol begs, but her mother holds her so tight. Alva Phillips, strong Alva, rocking too and chanting, *O Yes.* No, do not look.

Wade,
Sea of trouble all mingled with fire
Come on my brethren it's time to go higher
Wade wade

The voices in great humming waves, slow, slow (when did it become the humming?), everyone swaying with it too, moving like in slow waves and singing, and up where Eddie is, a new cry, wild and open, "O help me, Jesus," and when Carol opens her eyes she closes them again, quick, but still can see the new known face from school (not Eddie), the thrashing, writhing body struggling against the ushers with the look of grave and loving support on their faces, and hear the torn, tearing cry: "Don't take me away, life everlasting don't take me away."

And now the rhinestones in Parry's hair glitter wicked; the white hands of the ushers, fanning, foam in the air; the blue-painted waters of Jordan swell and thunder; Christ spirals on his cross in the window—and she is drowned under the sluice of the slow singing and the sway.

So high up and forgotten the waves and the world, so stirless the deep cool green and the wrecks of what had been. Here now Hostess Foods, where Alva Phillips works her nights—but different from that time Alva had taken them through before work, for it is all sunken under water, the creaking loading platform where they had left the night behind; the closet room where Alva's swaddles of sweaters, boots, and cap hung, the long hall lined with pickle barrels, the sharp freezer door swinging open.

Bubbles of breath that swell. A gulp of numbing air. She swims into the chill room where the huge wheels of cheese stand, and Alva swims too, deftly oiling each machine: slicers and wedgers and the convey, that at her touch start to roll and grind. The light of day blazes up and Alva is holding a cup, saying: Drink this, baby.

"DRINK IT." Her mother's voice and the numbing air demanding her to pay attention. Up through the waters and into the car.

"That's right, lambie, now lie back." Her mother's lap.

"Mother."

"Shhhhh. You almost fainted, lambie."

Alva's voice. "You gonna be all right, Carol . . . Lucy, I'm telling you for the last time, you and Buford get back into that church. Carol is *fine*."

"Lucyinda, if I had all your petticoats I could float." Crying. "Why didn't you let me wear my full skirt with the petticoats, Mother."

"Shhhhh, lamb." Smoothing her cheek. "Just breathe, take long deep breaths."

". . . How you doing now, you little ol' consolation prize?" It is Parry, but she does not come in the car or reach to Carol through the open window: "No need to cuss and fuss. You going to be sharp as a tack, Jack."

Answering automatically: "And cool as a fool."

Quick, they look at each other.

"Parry, we have to go home now, don't we, Mother? I almost fainted, didn't I, Mother? . . . Parry, I'm sorry I got sick and have to miss your baptism."

"Don't feel sorry. I'll feel better you not there to watch. It was our mommas wanted you to be there, not me."

"Parry!" Three voices.

"Maybe I'll come over to play kickball after. If you feeling better. Maybe. Or bring the pogo." Old shared joys in her voice. "Or any little thing."

In just a whisper: "Or any little thing. Parry. Good-bye, Parry."

And why does Alva have to talk now?

"You all right? You breathin' deep like your momma said? Was it too close 'n hot in there? Did something scare you, Carrie?"

Shaking her head to lie, "No."

"I blames myself for not paying attention. You not used to people letting go that way. Lucy and Bubbie, Parialee, they used to it. They been coming since they lap babies."

"Alva, that's all right. Alva. Mrs. Phillips."

"You *was* scared. Carol, it's something to study about. You'll feel better if you understand."

Trying not to listen.

"You not used to hearing what people keeps inside, Carol. You know how music can make you feel things? Glad or sad or like you can't sit still? That was religion music, Carol."

"I have to breathe deep, Mother said."

"Not everybody feels religion the same way. Some it's in their mouth, but some it's like a hope in their blood, their bones. And they singing songs every word that's real to them, Carol, every word out of they own life. And the preaching finding lodgment in their hearts."

The screaming was tuning up in her ears again, high above Alva's patient voice and the waves lapping and fretting.

"Maybe somebody's had a hard week, Carol, and they locked up with it. Maybe a lot of hard weeks bearing down."

"Mother, my head hurts."

"And they're home, Carol, church is home. Maybe the only place they can feel how they feel and maybe let it come out. So they can go on. And it's all right."

"Please, Alva. Mother, tell Alva my head hurts."

"Get Happy, we call it, and most it's a good feeling, Carol. When you got all that locked up inside you."

"Tell her we have to go home. It's all right, Alva. Please, Mother. Say good-bye. Good-bye."

When I was carrying Parry and her father left me, and I fifteen years old, one thousand miles away from home, sin-sick and never really believing, as still I don't believe all, scorning, for what have it done to help, waiting there in the clinic and maybe sleeping, a voice called: Alva, Alva. So mournful and so sweet: Alva. Fear not, I have loved you from the foundation of the universe. And a little small child tugged on my dress. He was carrying a parade stick, on the end of it a star that outshined the sun. Follow me, he said. And the real sun went down and he hidden his stick. How dark it was, how dark. I could feel the darkness with my hands. And when I could see, I screamed. Dump trucks run, dumping bodies in hell, and a convey line run, never ceasing with souls, weary ones having to stamp and shove them along, and the air like fire. Oh I never want to hear such screaming. Then the little child jumped on a motorbike making a path no bigger than my little finger. But first he greased my feet with the hands of my momma when I was a knee baby. They shined like the sun was on them. Eyes he placed all around my head, and as I journeyed upward after him, it seemed I heard a mourning: "Mama Mama you must help carry the world." The rise and fall of nations I saw. And the voice called again Alva Alva, and I flew into a world of light, multitudes singing, Free, free, I am so glad.

2

Helen began to cry, telling her husband about it.

"You and Alva ought to have your heads examined, taking her

there cold like that," Len said. "All right, wreck my best handkerchief. Anyway, now that she's had a bath, her Sunday dinner. . . ."

"And been fussed over," seventeen-year-old Jeannie put in.

"She seems good as new. Now *you* forget it, Helen."

"I can't. Something . . . deep happened. If only I or Alva had told her what it would be like. . . . But I didn't realize."

You don't realize a lot of things, Mother, Jeannie said, but not aloud.

"So Alva talked about it after instead of before. Maybe it meant more that way."

"Oh Len, she didn't listen."

"You don't know if she did or not. Or what there was in the experience for her. . . ."

Enough to pull that kid apart two ways even more, Jeannie said, but still not aloud.

"I was so glad she and Parry were going someplace together again. Now that'll be between them too. Len, they really need, miss each other. What happened in a few months? When I think of how close they were, the hours of makebelieve and dressup and playing ball and collecting. . . ."

"Grow up, Mother." Jeannie's voice was harsh. "Parialee's collecting something else now. Like her own crowd. Like jivetalk and rhythmandblues. Like teachers who treat her like a dummy and white kids who treat her like dirt; boys who think she's really something and chicks who. . . ."

"Jeannie, I know. It hurts."

"Well, maybe it hurts Parry too. Maybe. At least she's got a crowd. Just don't let it hurt Carol though, 'cause there's nothing she can do about it. That's all through, her and Parialee Phillips, put away with their paper dolls."

"No, Jeannie, no."

"It's like Ginger and me. Remember Ginger, my best friend in Horace Mann. But you hardly noticed when it happened to us, did you . . . because she was white? Yes, Ginger, who's got two kids now, who quit school year before last. Parry's never going to finish either. What's she got to do with Carrie any more? They're going different places. Different places, different crowds. And they're sorting. . . ."

"Now wait, Jeannie. Parry's just as bright, just as capable."

"They're in junior high, Mother. Don't you know about junior high? How they sort? And it's all where you're going. Yes and Parry's colored and Carrie's white. And you have to watch everything, what you wear and how you wear it and who you eat lunch with and how much homework you do and how you act to the teacher and what you laugh at. . . . And run with your crowd."

"It's that final?" asked Len. "Don't you think kids like Carol and Parry can show it doesn't *have* to be that way."

"They can't. They can't. They don't let you."

"No need to shout," he said mildly. "And who do you mean by 'they' and what do you mean by 'sorting'?"

How they sort. A foreboding of comprehension whirled within Helen. What was it Carol had told her of the Welcome Assembly the first day in junior high? The models showing How to Dress and How Not to Dress and half the girls in their loved new clothes watching their counterparts up on the stage—*their* straight skirt, their sweater, their earrings, lipstick, hairdo—"How Not to Dress," "a bad reputation for your school." It was nowhere in Carol's description, yet picturing it now, it seemed to Helen that a mute cry of violated dignity hung in the air. Later there had been a story of going to another Low 7 homeroom on an errand and seeing a teacher trying to wipe the forbidden lipstick off a girl who was fighting back and cursing. Helen could hear Carol's frightened, self-righteous tones: ". . . and I hope they expel her; she's the kind that gives Franklin Jr. a bad rep; she doesn't care about anything and always gets into fights." Yet there was nothing in these incidents to touch the heavy comprehension that waited. . . . Homework, the wonderings those times Jeannie and Carol needed help: "What if there's no one at home to give the help, and the teachers with their two hundred and forty kids a day can't or don't or the kids don't ask and they fall hopelessly behind, what then?"—but this too was unrelated. And what had it been that time about Parry? "Mother, Melanie and Sharon won't go if they know Parry's coming." Then of course you'll go with Parry, she's been your friend longer, she had answered, but where was it they were going and what had finally happened? Len, my head hurts, she felt like saying, in Carol's voice in the car, but Len's eyes were grave on Jeannie who was saying passionately:

"If you think it's so goddam important why do we have to live here where it's for real; why don't we move to Ivy like Betsy (yes, I know, money), where it's the deal to be buddies, in school anyway, three coloured kids and their father's a doctor or judge or something big wheel and one always gets elected President or head song girl or something to prove oh how we're democratic. . . . What do you want of that poor kid anyway? Make up your mind. Stay friends with Parry—but be one of the kids. Sure. Be a brain—but not a square. Rise on up, college prep, but don't get separated. Yes, stay one of the kids but. . . ."

"Jeannie. You're not talking about Carol at all, are you, Jeannie? Say it again. I wasn't listening. I was trying to think."

"She will not say it again," Len said firmly, "you look about ready to pull a Carol. One a day's our quota. And you, Jeannie, we'd better cool it. Too much to talk about for one session. . . . Here, come to the window and watch the Carol and Parry you're both all worked up about."

In the wind and the shimmering sunset light, half the children of the block are playing down the street. Leaping, bouncing, hallooing, tugging the kites of spring. In the old synchronized understanding, Carol and Parry kick, catch, kick, catch. And now Parry jumps on her pogo stick (the last time), Carol shadowing her, and Bubbie, arching his body in a semicircle of joy, bounding after them, high, higher, higher.

And the months go by and supposedly it is forgotten, except for the now and then when, self-important, Carol will say: I really truly did nearly faint, didn't I, Mother, that time I went to church with Parry?

And now seldom Parry and Carol walk the hill together. Melanie's mother drives by to pick up Carol, and the several times Helen has suggested Parry, too, Carol is quick to explain: "She's already left" or "She isn't ready; she'll make us late."

And after school? Carol is off to club or skating or library or someone's house, and Parry can stay for kickball only on the rare afternoons when she does not have to hurry home where Lucy, Bubbie, and the cousins wait to be cared for, now Alva works the four to twelve-thirty shift.

No more the bending together over the homework. All semester the teachers have been different, and rarely Parry brings her books home, for where is there space or time and what is the sense? And the phone never rings with: what you going to wear tomorrow, are you bringing your lunch, or come on over, let's design some clothes for the Katy Keane comic-book contest. And Parry never drops by with Alva for Saturday snack to or from grocery shopping.

And the months go by and the sorting goes on and seemingly it is over until that morning when Helen must stay home from work, so swollen and feverish is Carol with mumps.

The afternoon before, Parry had come by, skimming up the stairs, spilling books and binders on the bed: Hey frail, looka-here and wail, your momma askin for homework, what she got against YOU? . . . looking quickly once then not looking again and talking fast. . . . Hey, you bloomed. You gonna be your own pumpkin, hallowe'en? Your momma know yet it's mu-umps? And lumps. Momma says: no distress, she'll be by tomorrow morning see do you need anything while your momma's to work. . . . (Singing: *whole lotta shakin goin on*.) All your 'signments is inside; Miss Rockface says the teachers to write 'em cause I mightn't get it right all right.

  But did not tell: Does your mother work for Carol's mother? Oh, you're neighbors! Very well, I'll send along a monitor to open Carol's locker but you're only to take these things I'm writing down, nothing else. Now say after me: Miss Campbell is trusting me to be a good responsible girl. And go right to Carol's house. After school. Not stop anywhere on the way. Not lose anything. And only take. What's written on the list.

You really gonna mess with that book stuff? Sign on *mine* says do-not-open-until-eX-mas. . . . That Mrs. Fernandez doll she didn't send nothin, she was the only, says feel better and read a book to report if you feel like and I'm the most for takin care for you; she's my most, wish I could get her but she only teaches 'celerated. . . . Flicking the old read books on the shelf but not opening to mock-declaim as once she used to . . . Vicky, Eddie's g.f. in Rockface office, she's on suspended for sure, yellin to Rockface: you bitchkitty don't you give me no more bad shit. That Vicky she can sure sling-ating-ring it. Staring out the window as if the tree not there in which they had hid out and rocked so often. . . . For sure. (*Keep mo-o-vin*.) Got me a new pink top and lilac skirt. Look sharp with this purple? Cinching in the wide belt as if delighted with what newly swelled above and swelled below. Wear it Saturday night to Sweet's, Modernaires Sounds of Joy, Leroy and Ginny and me goin if Momma'll stay home. IF. (*Shake my baby shake*). How come old folks still likes to party? Huh? Asking of Rembrandt's weary old face looking from the wall. How come (softly) you long-gone you. Touching her face to his quickly, lightly. NEXT mumps is your buddybud Melanie's turn to tote your stuff. *I'm* gettin the hoovus goovus. Hey you so un-neat, don't care what you bed with. Removing the books and binders, ranging them on the dresser one by one, marking lipstick faces—bemused or mocking or amazed—on each paper jacket. Better. Fluffing out smoothing the quilt with exaggerated energy. Any little thing I can get, cause I gotta blow. Tossing up and catching their year-ago, arm-in-arm graduation picture, replacing it deftly, upside down, into its mirror crevice. Joe. Bring you joy juice or fizz water or kickapoo? Adding a frown line to one bookface. Twanging the paper fishkite, the Japanese windbell overhead, setting the mobile they had once made of painted eggshells and decorated straws to twirling and rocking. And is gone.

She talked to the lipstick faces after, in her fever, tried to stand on her head to match the picture, twirled and twanged with the violent overhead.

Sleeping at last after the disordered night. Having surrounded herself with the furnishings of that world of childhood she no sooner learned to live in comfortably, then had to leave.

The dollhouse stands there to arrange and rearrange; the shell and picture card collections to re-sort and remember; the population of dolls given away to little sister, borrowed back, propped all around to dress and undress and caress.

She has thrown off her nightgown because of the fever, and her just budding breast is exposed where she reaches to hold the floppy plush dog that had been her childhood pillow.

Not for anything would Helen have disturbed her. Except that in the unaccustomedness of a morning at home, in the bruised restlessness after the sleepless night, she clicks on the radio—and the storm of singing whirls into the room:

> . . . *of trouble all mingled with fire*
> *Come on my brethren we've got to go higher*
> *Wade, wade. . . .*

And Carol runs down the stairs, shrieking and shrieking. "Turn it off, Mother, turn it off." Hurling herself at the dial and wrenching it so it comes off in her hand.

"Ohhhhh," choked and convulsive, while Helen tries to hold her, to quiet.

"Mother, why did they sing and scream like that?"

"At Parry's church?"

"Yes." Rocking and strangling the cries. "I hear it all the time." Clinging and beseeching. ". . . What was it, Mother? Why?"

Emotion, Helen thought of explaining, *a characteristic of the religion of all oppressed peoples, yes your very own great-grandparents*—thought of saying. And discarded.

Aren't you now, haven't you had feelings in yourself so strong they had to come out some way? ("what howls restrained by decorum")—thought of saying. And discarded.

Repeat Alva: *hope . . . every word out of their own life. A place to let go. And church is home.* And discarded.

The special history of the Negro people—history?—just you try living what must be lived every day—thought of saying. And discarded.

And said nothing.

And said nothing.

And soothed and held.

"Mother, a lot of the teachers and kids don't like Parry when they don't even know what she's like. Just because . . ." Rocking again, convulsive and shamed. "And I'm not really her friend any more."

No news. Betrayal and shame. Who betrayed? Whose shame? Brought herself to say aloud: "But maybe friends again. As Alva and I are."

The sobbing a whisper. "That girl Vicky who got that way when I fainted, she's in school. She's the one keeps wearing the lipstick and they wipe it off and she's always in trouble and now maybe she's expelled. Mother."

"Yes, lambie."

"She acts so awful outside but I remember how she was in church and whenever I see her now I have to wonder. And hear . . . like I'm her, Mother, like I'm her." Clinging and trembling. "Oh why do I have to feel it's happening to me too?

"Mother, I want to forget about it all, and not care,—like Melanie. Why can't I forget? Oh why is it like it is and why do I have to care?"

Caressing, quieting.

Thinking: *caring asks doing. It is a long baptism into the seas of humankind, my daughter. Better immersion than to live untouched. . . . Yet how will you sustain?*

Why is it like it is?

Sheltering her daughter close, mourning the illusion of the embrace.

And why do I have to care?

While in her, her own need leapt and plunged for the place of strength that was not—where one could scream or sorrow while all knew and accepted, and gloved and loving hands waited to support and understand.

1956

For Margaret Heaton, who always taught

TELL ME A RIDDLE

I

For forty-seven years they had been married. How deep back the stubborn, gnarled roots of the quarrel reached, no one could say—but only now, when tending to the needs of others no longer shackled them together, the roots swelled up visible, split the earth between them, and the tearing shook even to the children, long since grown.

Why now, why now? wailed Hannah.

As if when we grew up weren't enough, said Paul.

Poor Ma. Poor Dad. It hurts so for both of them, said Vivi. They never had very much; at least in old age they should be happy.

Knock their heads together, insisted Sammy; tell 'em: you're too old for this kind of thing; no reason not to get along now.

Lennie wrote to Clara: They've lived over so much together; what could possibly tear them apart?

Something tangible enough.

Arthritic hands, and such work as he got, occasional. Poverty all his life, and there was little breath left for running. He could not, could not turn away from this desire: to have the troubling of responsibility, the fretting with money, over and done with; to be free, to be *care*free where success was not measured by accumulation, and there was use for the vitality still in him.

There was a way. They could sell the house, and with the money join his lodge's Haven, cooperative for the aged. Happy communal life, and was he not already an official; had he not helped organize it, raise funds, served as a trustee?

But she—would not consider it.

"What do we need all this for?" he would ask loudly, for her hearing aid was turned down and the vacuum was shrilling. "Five rooms" (pushing the sofa so she could get into the corner) "furniture" (smoothing down the rug) "floors and surfaces to make work. Tell me, why do we need it?" And he was glad he could ask in a scream.

"Because I'm use't."

"Because you're use't. This is a reason, Mrs. Word Miser? Used to can get unused!"

"Enough unused I have to get used to already. . . . Not enough words?" turning off the vacuum a moment to hear herself answer. "Because soon enough we'll need only a little closet, no windows, no furniture, nothing to make work, but for worms. Because now I want room. . . . Screech and blow like you're doing, you'll need that closet even sooner. . . . Ha, again!" for the vacuum bag wailed, puffed half up, hung stubbornly limp. "This time fix it so it stays; quick before the phone rings and you get too important-busy."

But while he struggled with the motor, it seethed in him. Why fix it? Why have to bother? And if it can't be fixed, have to wring the mind with how to pay the repair? At the Haven they come in with their own machines to clean your room or your cottage; you fish, or play cards, or make jokes in the sun, not with knotty fingers fight to mend vacuums.

Over the dishes, coaxingly: "For once in your life, to be free, to have everything done for you, like a queen."

"I never liked queens."

"No dishes, no garbage, no towel to sop, no worry what to buy, what to eat."

"And what else would I do with my empty hands? Better to eat at my own table when I want, and to cook and eat how I want."

"In the cottages they buy what you ask, and cook it how you like. *You* are the one who always used to say: better mankind born without mouths and stomachs than always to worry for money to buy, to shop, to fix, to cook, to wash, to clean."

"How cleverly you hid that you heard. I said it then because eighteen hours a day I ran. And you never scraped a carrot or knew a dish towel sops. Now—for you and me—who cares? A herring out of a jar is enough. But when *I* want, and nobody to bother." And she turned off her ear button, so she would not have to hear.

But as *he* had no peace, juggling and rejuggling the money to figure: how will I pay for this now?; prying out the storm windows (there they take care of this); jolting in the streetcar on errands (there I would not have to ride to take care of this or that); fending the patronizing relatives just back from Florida (at the Haven it matters what one is, not what one can afford), he gave *her* no peace.

"Look! In their bulletin. A reading circle. Twice a week it meets."

"Haumm," her answer of not listening.

"A reading circle. Chekhov they read that you like, and Peretz. Cultured people at the Haven that you would enjoy."

"Enjoy!" She tasted the word. "Now, when it pleases you, you find a reading circle for me. And forty years ago when the children were morsels and there was a Circle, did you stay home with them once so I could go? Even once? You trained me well. I do not need others to enjoy. Others!" Her voice trembled. "Because *you* want to be there with others. Already it makes me sick to think of you always around others. Clown, grimacer, floormat, yesman, entertainer, whatever they want of you."

And now it was he who turned on the television loud so he need not hear.

Old scar tissue ruptured and the wounds festered anew. Chekhov indeed. She thought without softness of that young wife, who in the deep night hours while she nursed the current baby, and perhaps held another in her lap, would try to stay awake for the only time there was to read. She would feel again the weather of the outside on his cheek when, coming late from a meeting, he would find her so, and stimulated and ardent, sniffing her skin, coax: "I'll put the baby to bed, and you—put the book away, don't read, don't read."

That had been the most beguiling of all the "don't read, put your book away" her life had been. Chekhov indeed!

"Money?" She shrugged him off. "Could we get poorer than once we were? And in America, who starves?"

But as still he pressed:

"Let me alone about money. Was there ever enough? Seven little ones—for every penny I had to ask—and sometimes, remember, there was nothing. But always *I* had to manage. Now *you* manage. Rub your nose in it good."

But from those years she had had to manage, old humiliations and terrors rose up, lived again, and forced her to relive them. The children's needings; that grocer's face or this merchant's wife she had had to beg credit from when credit was a disgrace; the scenery of the long blocks walked around when she could not pay; school coming, and the desperate going over the old to see what could yet be remade; the soups of meat bones begged "for-the-dog" one winter. . . .

Enough. Now they had no children. Let *him* wrack his head for how they would live. She would not exchange her solitude for anything. *Never again to be forced to move to the rhythms of others.*

For in this solitude she had won to a reconciled peace.

Tranquility from having the empty house no longer an enemy, for it stayed clean—not as in the days when it was her family, the life in it, that had seemed the enemy: tracking, smudging, littering, dirtying, engaging her in endless defeating battle—and on whom her endless defeat had been spewed.

The few old books, memorized from rereading; the pictures to ponder (the magnifying glass superimposed on her heavy eyeglasses). Or if she wishes, when he is gone, the phonograph, that if she turns up very loud and strains, she can hear: the ordered sounds and the struggling.

Out in the garden, growing things to nurture. Birds to be kept out of the pear tree, and when the pears are heavy and ripe, the old fury of work, for all must be canned, nothing wasted.

And her one social duty (for she will not go to luncheons or meetings) the boxes of old clothes left with her, as with a life-practised eye for finding what is still wearable within the worn (again the magnifying glass superimposed on the heavy glasses) she scans and sorts—this for rag or rummage, that for mending and cleaning, and this for sending away.

Being able at last to live within, and not move to the rhythms of others, as life had forced her to: denying; removing; isolating; taking the children one by one; then deafening, half-blinding—and at last, presenting her solitude.

And in it she had won to a reconciled peace.

Now he was violating it with his constant campaigning: *Sell the house and move to the Haven.* (You sit, you sit—there too you could sit like a stone.) He was making of her a battleground where old grievances tore. (Turn on your ear button—I am talking.) And stubbornly she resisted—so that from wheedling, reasoning, manipulation, it was bitterness he now started with.

And it came to where every happening lashed up a quarrel.

"I will sell the house anyway," he flung at her one night. "I am putting it up for sale. There will be a way to make you sign."

The television blared, as always it did on the evenings he stayed home, and as always it reached her only as noise. She did not know if the tumult was in her or outside. Snap! she turned the sound off. "Shadows," she whispered to him, pointing to the screen, "look, it is only shadows." And in a scream: "Did you say that you will sell the house? Look at me, not at that. I am no shadow. You cannot sell without me."

"Leave on the television. I am watching."

"Like Paulie, like Jenny, a four-year-old. Staring at shadows. *You cannot sell the house.*"

"I will. We are going to the Haven. There you would not hear the television when you do not want it. I could sit in the social room and watch. You could lock yourself up to smell your unpleasantness in a room by yourself—for who would want to come near you?"

"No, no selling." A whisper now.

"The television is shadows. Mrs. Enlightened! Mrs. Cultured! A world comes into your house—and it is shadows. People you would never meet in a thousand lifetimes. Wonders. When you were four years old, yes, like Paulie, like Jenny, did you know of Indian dances, alligators, how they use bamboo in Malaya? No, you scratched in your dirt with the chickens and thought Olshana was the world. Yes, Mrs. Unpleasant, I will sell the house, for there better can we be rid of each other than here."

She did not know if the tumult was outside, or in her. Always a ravening inside, a pull to the bed, to lie down, to succumb.

"Have you thought maybe Ma should let a doctor have a look at her?" asked their son Paul after Sunday dinner, regarding his mother crumpled on the couch, instead of, as was her custom, busying herself in Nancy's kitchen.

"Why not the President too?"

"Seriously, Dad. This is the third Sunday she's lain down like that after dinner. Is she that way at home?"

"A regular love affair with the bed. Every time I start to talk to her."

Good protective reaction, observed Nancy to herself. The workings of hos-til-ity.

"Nancy could take her. I just don't like how she looks. Let's have Nancy arrange an appointment."

"You think she'll go?" regarding his wife gloomily. "All right, we have to have doctor bills, we have to have doctor bills." Loudly: "Something hurts you?"

She startled, looked to his lips. He repeated: "Mrs. Take It Easy, something hurts?"

"Nothing. . . . Only you."

"A woman of honey. That's why you're lying down?"

"Soon I'll get up to do the dishes, Nancy."

"Leave them, Mother, I like it better this way."

"Mrs. Take It Easy, Paul says you should start ballet. You should go to see a doctor and ask: how soon can you start ballet?"

"A doctor?" she begged. "Ballet?"

"We were talking, Ma," explained Paul, "you don't seem any too well. It would be a good idea for you to see a doctor for a checkup."

"I get up now to do the kitchen. Doctors are bills and foolishness, my son. I need no doctors."

"At the Haven," he could not resist pointing out, "a doctor is *not* bills. He lives beside you. You start to sneeze, he is there before you open up a Kleenex. You can be sick there for free, all you want."

"Diarrhea of the mouth, is there a doctor to make you dumb?"

"Ma. Promise me you'll go. Nancy will arrange it."

"It's all of a piece when you think of it," said Nancy, "the way she attacks my kitchen, scrubbing under every cup hook, doing the inside of the oven so I can't enjoy Sunday dinner, knowing that half-blind or not, she's going to find every speck of dirt. . . ."

"Don't, Nancy, I've told you—it's the only way she knows to be useful. What did the *doctor* say?"

"A real fatherly lecture. Sixty-nine is young these days. Go out, enjoy life, find interests. Get a new hearing aid, this one is antiquated. Old age is sickness only if one makes it so. Geriatrics, Inc."

"So there was nothing physical."

"Of course there was. How can you live to yourself like she does without there being? Evidence of a kidney disorder, and her blood count is low. He gave her a diet, and she's to come back for follow-up and lab work. . . . But he was clear enough: Number One prescription—start living like a human being. . . . When I think of your dad, who could really play the invalid with that arthritis of his, as active as a teenager, and twice as much fun. . . ."

"You didn't tell me the doctor says your sickness is in you, how you live." He pushed his advantage. "Life and enjoyments you need better than medicine. And this diet, how can you keep it? To weigh each morsel and scrape away each bit of fat, to make this soup, that pudding. There, at the Haven, they have a dietician, they would do it for you.

She is silent.

"You would feel better there, I know it," he says gently. "There there is life and enjoyments all around."

"What is the matter, Mr. Importantbusy, you have no card game or meeting you can go to?"—turning her face to the pillow.

For a while he cut his meetings and going out, fussed over her diet, tried to wheedle her into leaving the house, brought in visitors:

"I should come to a fashion tea. I should sit and look at pretty babies in clothes I cannot buy. This is pleasure?"
"Always you are better than everyone else. The doctor said you should go out. Mrs. Brem comes to you with goodness and you turn her away."
"Because *you* asked her to, she asked me."

"They won't come back. People you need, the doctor said. Your own cousins I asked; they were willing to come and make peace as if nothing had happened. . . ."

"No more crushers of people, pushers, hypocrites, around me. No more in *my* house. You go to them if you like."

"Kind he is to visit. And you, like ice."

"A babbler. All my life around babblers. Enough!"

"She's even worse, Dad? Then let her stew a while," advised Nancy. "You can't let it destroy you; it's a psychological thing, maybe too far gone for any of us to help."

So he let her stew. More and more she lay silent in bed, and sometimes did not even get up to make the meals. No longer was the tongue-lashing inevitable if he left the coffee cup where it did not belong, or forgot to take out the garbage or mislaid the broom. The birds grew bold that summer and for once pocked the pears, undisturbed.

A bellyful of bitterness and every day the same quarrel in a new way and a different old grievance the quarrel forced her to enter and relive. And the new torment: I am not really sick, the doctor said it, then why do I feel so sick?

One night she asked him: "You have a meeting tonight? Do not go. Stay . . . with me."

He had planned to watch "This Is Your Life," but half sick himself from the heavy heat, and sickening therefore the more after the brooks and woods of the Haven, with satisfaction he grated:

"Hah, Mrs. Live Alone And Like It wants company all of a sudden. It doesn't seem so good the time of solitary when she was a girl exile in Siberia. 'Do not go. Stay with me.' A new song for Mrs. Free As A Bird. Yes, I am going out, and while I am gone chew this aloneness good, and think how you keep us both from where if you want people, you do not need to be alone."

"Go, go. All your life you have gone without me."

After him she sobbed curses he had not heard in years, old-country curses from their childhood: Grow, oh shall you grow like an onion, with your head in the ground. Like the hide of a drum shall you be, beaten in life, beaten in death. Oh shall you be like a chandelier, to hang, and to burn. . . .

She was not in their bed when he came back. She lay on the cot on the sun porch. All week she did not speak or come near him; nor did he try to make peace or care for her.

He slept badly, so used to her next to him. After all the years, old harmonies and dependencies deep in their bodies; she curled to him, or he coiled to her, each warmed, warming, turning as the other turned, the nights a long embrace.

It was not the empty bed or the storm that woke him, but a faint singing. *She* was singing. Shaking off the drops of rain, the lightning riving her lifted face, he saw her so; the cot covers on the floor.

"This is a private concert?" he asked. "Come in, you are wet."

"I can breathe now," she answered; "my lungs are rich." Though indeed the sound was hardly a breath.

"Come in, come in." Loosing the bamboo shades. "Look how wet you are." Half helping, half carrying her, still faint-breathing her song.

A Russian love song of fifty years ago.

He had found a buyer, but before he told her, he called together those children who were close enough to come. Paul, of course, Sammy from New Jersey, Hannah from Connecticut, Vivi from Ohio.

With a kindling of energy for her beloved visitors, she arrayed the house, cooked and baked. She was not prepared for the solemn after-dinner conclave, they too probing in and tearing. Her frightened eyes watched from mouth to mouth as each spoke.

His stories were eloquent and funny of her refusal to go back to the doctor; of the scorned invitations; of her stubborn silence or the bile "like a Niagara"; of her contrariness: "If I clean it's no good how I cleaned; if I don't clean, I'm still a master who thinks he has a slave."

(Vinegar he poured on me all his life; I am well marinated; how can I be honey now?)

Deftly he marched in the rightness for moving to the Haven; their money from social security free for visiting the children, not sucked into daily needs and into the house; the activities in the Haven for him; but mostly the Haven for *her*: her health, her need of care, distraction, amusement, friends who shared her interests.

"This does offer an outlet for Dad," said Paul; "he's always been an active person. And economic peace of mind isn't to be sneezed at, either. I could use a little of that myself."

But when they asked: "And you, Ma, how do you feel about it?" could only whisper:

"For him it is good. It is not for me. I can no longer live between people."

"You lived all your life *for* people," Vivi cried.

"Not with." Suffering doubly for the unhappiness on her children's faces.

"You have to find some compromise," Sammy insisted. "Maybe sell the house and buy a trailer. After forty-seven years there's surely some way you can find to live in peace."

"There is no help, my children. Different things we need."

"Then live alone!" He could control himself no longer. "I have a buyer for the house. Half the money for you, half for me. Either alone or with me to the Haven. You think I can live any longer as we are doing now?"

"Ma doesn't have to make a decision this minute, however you feel, Dad," Paul said quickly, "and you wouldn't want her to. Let's let it lay a few months, and then talk some more."

"I think I can work it out to take Mother home with me for a while," Hannah said. "You both look terrible, but especially you, Mother. I'm going to ask Phil to have a look at you."

"Sure," cracked Sammy. "What's the use of a doctor husband if you can't get free service out of him once in a while for the family? And absence might make the heart . . . you know."

"There was something after all," Paul told Nancy in a colorless voice. "That was Hannah's Phil calling. Her gall bladder. . . . Surgery."

"Her *gall* bladder. If that isn't classic. 'Bitter as gall'—talk of psychosom—"

He stepped closer, put his hand over her mouth, and said in the same colorless, plodding voice. "We have to get Dad. They operated at once. The cancer was everywhere, surrounding the liver, every-where. They did what they could . . . at best she has a year. Dad . . . we have to tell him."

2

Honest in his weakness when they told him, and that she was not to know. "I'm not an actor. She'll know right away by how I am. Oh that poor woman. I am old too, it will break me into pieces. Oh that poor woman. She will spit on me: 'So my sickness was how I live.' Oh Paulie, how she will be, that poor woman. Only she should not suffer. . . . I can't stand sickness, Paulie, I can't go with you."

But went. And play-acted.

"A grand opening and you did not even wait for me. . . . A good thing Hannah took you with her."

"Fashion teas I needed. They cut out what tore in me; just in my throat something hurts yet. . . . Look! so many flowers, like a funeral. Vivi called, did Hannah tell you? And Lennie from San Francisco, and Clara; and Sammy is coming." Her gnome's face pressed happily into the flowers.

It is impossible to predict in these cases, but once over the immediate effects of the operation, she should have several months of comparative well-being.

68

The money, where will come the money?

Travel with her, Dad. Don't take her home to the old associations. The other children will want to see her.

The money, where will I wring the money?

Whatever happens, she is not to know. No, you can't ask her to sign papers to sell the house; nothing to upset her. Borrow instead, then after. . . .

I had wanted to leave you each a few dollars to make life easier, as other fathers do. There will be nothing left now. (Failure! you and your "business is exploitation." Why didn't you make it when it could be made?—Is that what you're thinking, Sammy?)

Sure she's unreasonable, Dad—but you have to stay with her; if there's to be any happiness in what's left of her life, it depends on you.

Prop me up, children, think of me, too. Shuffled, chained with her, bitter woman. No Haven, and the little money going. . . . How happy she looks, poor creature.

The look of excitement. The straining to hear everything (the new hearing aid turned full). Why are you so happy, dying woman?

How the petals are, fold on fold, and the gladioli color. The autumn air.

Stranger grandsons, tall above the little gnome grandmother, the little spry grandfather. Paul in a frenzy of picture-taking before going.

She, wandering the great house. Feeling the books; laughing at the maple shoemaker's bench of a hundred years ago used as a table. The ear turned to music.

"Let us go home. See how good I walk now." "One step from the hospital," he answers, "and she wants to fly. Wait till Doctor Phil says."

"Look—the birds too are flying home. Very good Phil is and will not show it, but he is sick of sickness by the time he comes home."

"Mrs. Telepathy, to read minds," he answers; "read mine what it says: when the trunks of medicines become a suitcase, then we will go."

The grandboys, they do not know what to say to us. . . . Hannah, she runs around here, there, when is there time for herself?

Let us go home. Let us go home.

Musing; gentleness—*but for the incidents of the rabbi in the hospital, and of the candles of benediction.*

Of the rabbi in the hospital:

Now tell me what happened, Mother.

From the sleep I awoke, Hannah's Phil, and he stands there like a devil in a dream and calls me by name. I cannot hear. I think he prays. Go away, please, I tell him, I am not a believer. Still he stands, while my heart knocks with fright.

You scared *him*, Mother. He thought you were delirious.

Who sent him? Why did he come to *me?*

It is a custom. The men of God come to visit those of their religion they might help. The hospital makes up the list for them—race, religion—and you are on the Jewish list.

Not for rabbis. At once go and make them change. Tell them to write: Race, human; Religion, none.

And of the candles of benediction:

Look how you have upset yourself, Mrs. Excited Over Nothing. Pleasant memories you should leave.

Go in, go back to Hannah and the lights. Two weeks I saw candles and said nothing. But she asked me.

So what was so terrible? She forgets you never did, she asks you to light the Friday candles and say the benediction like Phil's mother when she visits. If the candles give her pleasure, why shouldn't she have the pleasure?

Not for pleasure she does it. For emptiness. Because his family does. Because all around her do.

That is not a good reason too? But you did not hear her. For heritage, she told you. For the boys, from the past they should have tradition.

Superstition! From our ancestors, savages, afraid of the dark, of themselves: mumbo words and magic lights to scare away ghosts.

She told you: how it started does not take away the goodness. For centuries, peace in the house it means.

Swindler! does she look back on the dark centuries? Candles bought instead of bread and stuck into a potato for a candlestick? Religion that stifled and said: in Paradise, woman, you will be the footstool of your husband, and in life—poor chosen Jew—ground under, despised, trembling in cellars. And cremated. And cremated.

This is religion's fault? You think you are still an orator of the 1905 revolution? Where are the pills for quieting? Which are they?

Heritage. How have we come from our savage past, how no longer to be savages—this to teach. To look back and learn what human-izes—this to teach. To smash all ghettos that divide us—not to go back, not to go back—this to teach. Learned books in the house, will humankind live or die, and she gives to her boys—superstition.

Hannah that is so good to you. Take your pill, Mrs. Excited For Nothing, swallow.

Heritage! But when did I have time to teach? Of Hannah I asked only hands to help.

Swallow.

Otherwise—musing; gentleness.

Not to travel. To go home.

The children want to see you. We have to show them you are as thorny a flower as ever.

Not to travel.

Vivi wants you should see her new baby. She sent the tickets—airplane tickets—a Mrs. Roosevelt she wants to make of you. To Vivi's we have to go.

A new baby. How many warm, seductive babies. She holds him stiffly, *away* from her, so that he wails. And a long shudder begins, and the sweat beads on her forehead.

"Hush, shush," croons the grandfather, lifting him back. "You should forgive your grandmamma, little prince, she has never held a baby before, only seen them in glass cases. Hush, shush."

"You're tired, Ma," says Vivi. "The travel and the noisy dinner. I'll take you to lie down."

(*A long travel from, to, what the feel of a baby evokes.*)

In the airplane, cunningly designed to encase from motion (no wind, no feel of flight), she had sat severely and still, her face turned to the sky through which they cleaved and left no scar.

So this was how it looked, the determining, the crucial sky, and this was how man moved through it, remote above the dwindled earth, the concealed human life. Vulnerable life, that could scar.

There was a steerage ship of memory that shook across a great, circular sea: clustered, ill human beings; and through the thick-stained air, tiny fretting waters in a window round like the airplane's—sun round, moon round. (The round thatched roofs of Olshana.) Eye round—like the smaller window that framed distance the solitary year of exile when only her eyes could travel, and no voice spoke. And the polar winds hurled themselves across snows trackless and endless and white—like the clouds which had closed together below and hidden the earth.

Now they put a baby in her lap. Do not ask me, she would have liked to beg. Enough the worn face of Vivi, the remembered grandchildren. I cannot, cannot. . . .

Cannot what? Unnatural grandmother, not able to make herself embrace a baby.

She lay there in the bed of the two little girls, her new hearing aid turned full, listening to the sound of the children going to sleep, the baby's fretful crying and hushing, the clatter of dishes being washed and put away. They thought she slept. Still she rode on.

It was not that she had not loved her babies, her children. The love—the passion of tending—had risen with the need like a torrent; and like a torrent drowned and immolated all else. But when the need was done—oh the power that was lost in the painful damming back and drying up of what still surged, but had nowhere to go. Only the thin pulsing left that could not quiet, suffering over lives one felt, but could no longer hold nor help.

On that torrent she had borne them to their own lives, and the riverbed was desert long years now. Not there would she dwell, a memoried wraith. Surely that was not all, surely there was more. Still the springs, the springs were in her seeking. Somewhere an older power that beat for life. Somewhere coherence, transport, meaning. If they would but leave her in the air now stilled of clamor, in the reconciled solitude, to journey on to herself.

And they put a baby in her lap. Immediacy to embrace, and the breath of *that* past: warm flesh like this that had claims and nuzzled away all else and with lovely mouths devoured; hot-living like an animal—intensely and now; the turning maze; the long drunkenness; the drowning into needing and being needed. Severely she looked back—and the shudder seized her again, and the sweat. Not that way. Not there, not now could she, not yet. . . .

And all that visit, she could not touch the baby.

"Daddy, is it the . . . sickness she's like that?" asked Vivi. "I was so glad to be having the baby—for her. I told Tim, it'll give her more happiness than anything, being around a baby again. And she hasn't played with him once."

He was not listening, "Aahh little seed of life, little charmer," he crooned, "Hollywood should see you. A heart of ice you would melt.

Kick, kick. The future you'll have for a ball. In 2050 still kick. Kick for your granddaddy then."

Attentive with the older children; sat through their performances (command performance; we command you to be the audience); helped Ann sort autumn leaves to find the best for a school program; listened gravely to Richard tell about his rock collection, while her lips mutely formed the words to remember: *igneous, sedimentary, metamorphic;* looked for missing socks, books, and bus tickets; watched the children whoop after their grandfather who knew how to tickle, chuck, lift, toss, do tricks, tell secrets, make jokes, match riddle for riddle. (Tell me a riddle, Grammy. I know no riddles, child.) Scrubbed sills and woodwork and furniture in every room; folded the laundry; straightened drawers; emptied the heaped baskets waiting for ironing (while he or Vivi or Tim nagged: You're supposed to rest here, you've been sick) but to none tended or gave food—and could not touch the baby.

After a week she said: "Let us go home. Today call about the tickets."

"You have important business, Mrs. Inahurry? The President waits to consult with you?" He shouted, for the fear of the future raced in him. "The clothes are still warm from the suitcase, your children cannot show enough how glad they are to see you, and you want home. There is plenty of time for home. We cannot be with the children at home."

"Blind to around you as always: the little ones sleep four in a room because we take their bed. We are two more people in a house with a new baby, and no help."

"Vivi is happy so. The children should have their grandparents a while, she told to me. I should have my mommy and daddy. . . ."

"Babbler and blind. Do you look at her so tired? How she starts to talk and she cries? I am not strong enough yet to help. Let us go home."

(To reconciled solitude.)

For it seemed to her the crowded noisy house was listening to her, listening for her. She could feel it like a great ear pressed under her heart. And everything knocked: quick constant raps: let me in, let me in.

How was it that soft reaching tendrils also became blows that knocked?

C'mon, Grandma, I want to show you. . . .

Tell me a riddle, Grandma. (*I know no riddles.*)

Look, Grammy, he's so dumb he can't even find his hands. (Dody and the baby on a blanket over the fermenting autumn mould.)

I made them—for you. (Ann) (Flat paper dolls with aprons that lifted on scalloped skirts that lifted on flowered pants; hair of yarn and great ringed questioning eyes.)

Watch me, Grandma. (Richard snaking up the tree, hanging exultant, free, with one hand at the top. Below Dody hunching over in pretend-cooking.) (*Climb too, Dody, climb and look.*)

Be my nap bed, Grammy. (The "No!" too late.)

Morty's abandoned heaviness, while his fingers ladder up and down her hearing-aid cord to his drowsy chant: eentsiebeentsiespider. (*Children trust.*)

It's to start off your own rock collection, Grandma. That's a trilobite fossil, 200 million years old (millions of years on a boy's mouth) and that one's obsidian, black glass.

Knocked and knocked.

Mother, I *told* you the teacher said we had to bring it back all filled out this morning. Didn't you even ask Daddy? Then tell *me* which plan and I'll check it: evacuate or stay in the city or wait for you to come and take me away. (Seeing the look of straining to hear.) It's for Disaster, Grandma. (*Children trust.*)

Vivi in the maze of the long, the lovely drunkenness. The old old noises: baby sounds; screaming of a mother flayed to exasperation; children quarreling; children playing; singing; laughter.

And Vivi's tears and memories, spilling so fast, half the words not understood.

She had started remembering out loud deliberately, so her mother would know the past was cherished, still lived in her.

Nursing the baby: My friends marvel, and I tell them, oh it's easy to be such a cow. I remember how beautiful my mother seemed nursing my brother, and the milk just flows. . . . Was that Davy? It must have been Davy. . . .

Lowering a hem: How did you ever . . . when I think how you made everything we wore . . . Tim, just think, seven kids and Mommy sewed everything . . . do I remember you sang while you sewed? That white dress with the red apples on the skirt you fixed over for me, was it Hannah's or Clara's before it was mine?

Washing sweaters: Ma, I'll never forget, one of those days so nice you washed clothes outside; one of the first spring days it must have been. The bubbles just danced while you scrubbed, and we chased after, and you stopped to show us how to blow our own bubbles with green onion stalks . . . you always. . . .

"Strong onion, to still make you cry after so many years," her father said, to turn the tears into laughter.

While Richard bent over his homework: Where is it now, do we still have it, the Book of the Martyrs? It always seemed so, well— exalted, when you'd put it on the round table and we'd all look at it together; there was even a halo from the lamp. The lamp with the beaded fringe you could move up and down; they're in style again, pulley lamps like that, but without the fringe. You know the book I'm talking about, Daddy, the Book of the Martyrs, the first picture was a bust of Spartacus . . . Socrates? I wish there was something like that for the children, Mommy, to give them what you. . . . (And the tears splashed again.)

(What I intended and did not? Stop it, daughter, stop it, leave that time. And he, the hypocrite, sitting there with tears in his eyes—it was nothing to you then, nothing.)

. . . The time you came to school and I almost died of shame because of your accent and because I knew you knew I was ashamed; how could I? . . . Sammy's harmonica and you danced to it once, yes you did, you and Davy squealing in your arms. . . . That time you bundled us up and walked us down to the railway station to stay the night 'cause it was heated and we didn't have any coal, that winter of the strike, you didn't think I remembered that, did you, Mommy? . . . How you'd call us out to see the sunsets. . . .

Day after day, the spilling memories. Worse now, questions, too. Even the grandchildren: Grandma, in the olden days, when you were little. . . .

It was the afternoons that saved.

While they thought she napped, she would leave the mosaic on the wall (of children's drawings, maps, calendars, pictures, Ann's cardboard dolls with their great ringed questioning eyes) and hunch in the girls' closet on the low shelf where the shoes stood, and the girls' dresses covered.

For that while she would painfully sheathe against the listening house, the tendrils and noises that knocked, and Vivi's spilling memories. Sometimes it helped to braid and unbraid the sashes that dangled, or to trace the pattern on the hoop slips.

Today she had jacks and children under jet trails to forget. Last night, Ann and Dody silhouetted in the window against the sunset of flaming man-made clouds of jet trail, their jacks ball accenting the peaceful noise of dinner being made. Had she told them, yes she had told them of how they played jacks in her village though there was no ball, no jacks. Six stones, round and flat, toss them out, the seventh on the back of the hand, toss, catch and swoop up as many as possible, toss again. . . .

Of stones (repeating Richard) there are three kinds: earth's fire jetting; rock of layered centuries; crucibled new out of the old (*igneous, sedimentary, metamorphic*). But there was that other—frozen to black glass, never to transform or hold the fossil memory . . . (let not my seed fall on stone). There was an ancient man who fought to heights a great rock that crashed back down eternally—eternal labor, freedom, labor . . . (stone will perish, but the word remain). And you, David, who with a stone slew, screaming: Lord, take my heart of stone and give me flesh.

Who was screaming? Why was she back in the common room of the prison, the sun motes dancing in the shafts of light, and the informer being brought in, a prisoner now, like themselves. And Lisa leaping, yes, Lisa, the gentle and tender, biting at the betrayer's jugular. Screaming and screaming.

No, it is the children screaming. Another of Paul and Sammy's terrible fights?

In Vivi's house. Severely: you are in Vivi's house.

Blows, screams, a call: "Grandma!" For her? Oh please not for her. Hide, hunch behind the dresses deeper. But a trembling little body hurls itself beside her—surprised, smothered laughter, arms surround her neck, tears rub dry on her cheek, and words too soft to understand whisper into her ear (Is this where you hide too, Grammy? It's my secret place, we have a secret now).

And the sweat beads, and the long shudder seizes.

It seemed the great ear pressed inside now, and the knocking. "We have to go home," she told him, "I grow ill here."

"It's your own fault, Mrs. Bodybusy, you do not rest, you do too much." He raged, but the fear was in his eyes. "It was a serious operation, they told you to take care. . . . All right, we will go to where you can rest."

But where? Not home to death, not yet. He had thought to Lennie's, to Clara's; beautiful visits with each of the children. She would have to rest first, be stronger. If they could but go to Florida—it glittered before him, the never-realized promise of Florida. California:

of course. (The money, the money, dwindling!) Los Angeles first for sun and rest, then to Lennie's in San Francisco.

He told her the next day. "You saw what Nancy wrote: snow and wind back home, a terrible winter. And look at you—all bones and a swollen belly. I called Phil: he said: 'A prescription, Los Angeles sun and rest.'"

She watched the words on his lips. "You have sold the house," she cried, "that is why we do not go home. That is why you talk no more of the Haven, why there is money for travel. After the children you will drag me to the Haven."

"The Haven! Who thinks of the Haven any more? Tell her, Vivi, tell Mrs. Suspicious: a prescription, sun and rest, to make you healthy. . . . And how could I sell the house without *you*?"

At the place of farewells and greetings, of winds of coming and winds of going, they say their good-byes.

They look back at her with the eyes of others before them: Richard with her own blue blaze; Ann with the nordic eyes of Tim; Morty's dreaming brown of a great-grandmother he will never know; Dody with the laughing eyes of him who had been her springtide love (who stands beside her now); Vivi's, all tears.

The baby's eyes are closed in sleep.

Good-bye, my children.

3

It is to the back of the great city he brought her, to the dwelling places of the cast-off old. Bounded by two lines of amusement piers to the north and to the south, and between a long straight paving rimmed with black benches facing the sand—sands so wide the ocean is only a far fluting.

In the brief vacation season, some of the boarded stores fronting the sands open, and families, young people and children, may be seen. A little tasseled tram shuttles between the piers, and the lights of roller coasters prink and tweak over those who come to have sensation made in them.

The rest of the year it is abandoned to the old, all else boarded up and still; seemingly empty, except the occasional days and hours when the sun, like a tide, sucks them out of the low rooming houses, casts them onto the benches and sandy rim of the walk—and sweeps them into decaying enclosures once again.

A few newer apartments glint among the low bleached squares. It is in one of these Lennie's Jeannie has arranged their rooms. "Only a few miles north and south people pay hundreds of dollars a month for just this gorgeous air, Grandaddy, just this ocean closeness."

She had been ill on the plane, lay ill for days in the unfamiliar room. Several times the doctor came by—left medicine she would not take. Several times Jeannie drove in the twenty miles from work, still in her Visiting Nurse uniform, the lightness and brightness of her like a healing.

"Who can believe it is winter?" he asked one morning. "Beautiful it is outside like an ad. Come, Mrs. Invalid, come to taste it. You are well enough to sit in here, you are well enough to sit outside. The doctor said it too."

But the benches were encrusted with people, and the sands at the sidewalk's edge. Besides, she had seen the far ruffle of the sea: "there take me," and though she leaned against him, it was she who led.

Plodding and plodding, sitting often to rest, he grumbling. Patting the sand so warm. Once she scooped up a handful, cradling it close to her better eye; peered, and flung it back. And as they came almost to the brink and she could see the glistening wet, she sat down, pulled off her shoes and stockings, left him and began to run. "You'll catch cold," he screamed, but the sand in his shoes weighed him down—he who had always been the agile one—and already the white spray creamed her feet.

He pulled her back, took a handkerchief to wipe off the wet and the sand. "Oh no," she said, "the sun will dry," seized the square and smoothed it flat, dropped on it a mound of sand, knotted the kerchief corners and tied it to a bag—"to look at with the strong glass" (for the first time in years explaining an action of hers)—and lay down with the little bag against her cheek, looking toward the shore that nurtured life as it first crawled toward consciousness the millions of years ago.

He took her one Sunday in the evil-smelling bus, past flat miles of blister houses, to the home of relatives. Oh what is this? she cried as the light began to smoke and the houses to dim and recede. Smog, he said, everyone knows but you. . . . Outside he kept his arms about her, but she walked with hands pushing the heavy air as if to open it, whispered: who has done this? sat down suddenly to vomit at the curb and for a long while refused to rise.

One's age as seen on the altered face of those known in youth. Is this they he has come to visit? This Max and Rose, smooth and pleasant, introducing them to polite children, disinterested grandchildren, "the whole family, once a month on Sundays. And why not? We have the room, the help, the food."

Talk of cars, of houses, of success: this son that, that daughter this. And *your* children? Hastily skimped over, the intermarriages, the obscure work—"my doctor son-in-law, Phil"—all he has to offer. She silent in a corner. (Car-sick like a baby, he explains.) Years since he has taken her to visit anyone but the children, and old apprehensions prickle: "no incidents," he silently begs, "no incidents." He itched to tell them. "A very sick woman," significantly, indicating her with his eyes, "a very sick woman." Their restricted faces did not react. "Have you thought maybe she'd do better at Palm Springs?" Rose asked. "Or at least a nicer section of the beach, nicer people, a pool." Not to have to say "money" he said instead: "would she have sand to look at through a magnifying glass?" and went on, detail after detail, the old habit betraying of parading the queerness of her for laughter.

After dinner—the others into the living room in men- or women-clusters, or into the den to watch TV—the four of them alone. She sat close to him, and did not speak. Jokes, stories, people they had known, beginning of reminiscence, Russia fifty-sixty years ago. Strange words across the Duncan Phyfe table: *hunger; secret meetings; human rights; spies; betrayals; prison; escape*—interrupted by one of the grandchildren: "Commercial's on; any Coke left? Gee, you're missing a real hair-raiser." And then a granddaughter (Max proudly: "look at her, an American queen") drove them home on her way back to U.C.L.A. No incident—except that there had been no incidents.

The first few mornings she had taken with her the magnifying glass, but he would sit only on the benches, so she rested at the foot, where slatted bench shadows fell, and unless she turned her hearing aid down, other voices invaded.

Now on the days when the sun shone and she felt well enough, he took her on the tram to where the benches ranged in oblongs, some with tables for checkers or cards. Again the blanket on the sand in the striped shadows, but she no longer brought the magnifying glass. He played cards, and she lay in the sun and looked towards the waters; or they walked—two blocks down to the scaling hotel, two blocks back—past chili-hamburger stands, open-doored bars, Next- to- New and perpetual rummage sale stores.

Once, out of the aimless walkers, slow and shuffling like themselves, someone ran unevenly towards them, embraced, kissed, wept: "dear friends, old friends." A friend of *hers*, not his: Mrs. Mays who had lived next door to them in Denver when the children were small.

Thirty years are compressed into a dozen sentences; and the present, not even in three. All is told: the children scattered; the husband dead; she lives in a room two blocks up from the sing hall—and points to the domed auditorium jutting before the pier. The leg? phlebitis; the heavy breathing? that, one does not ask. She, too, comes to the benches each day to sit. And tomorrow, tomorrow, are they going to the community sing? Of course he would have heard of it, everybody goes—the big doings they wait for all week. They have never been? She will come to them for dinner tomorrow and they will all go together.

So it is that she sits in the wind of the singing, among the thousand various faces of age.

She had turned off her hearing aid at once they came into the auditorium—as she would have wished to turn off sight.

One by one they streamed by and imprinted on her—and though the savage zest of their singing came voicelessly soft and distant, the faces still roared—the faces densened the air—chorded into

children-chants, mother-croons, singing of the chained love serenades, Beethoven storms, mad Lucia's scream drunken joy-songs, keens for the dead, work-singing

while from floor to balcony to dome a bare-footed sore-covered little girl threaded the sound-thronged tumult, danced her ecstasy of grimace to flutes that scratched at a cross-roads village wedding
Yes, faces became sound, and the sound became faces; and faces and sound became weight—pushed, pressed

"Air"—her hands claw his.

"Whenever I enjoy myself. . . ." Then he saw the gray sweat on her face. "Here. Up. Help me, Mrs. Mays," and they support her out to where she can gulp the air in sob after sob.

"A doctor, we should get for her a doctor."

"Tch, it's nothing," says Ellen Mays, "I get it all the time. You've missed the tram; come to my place. Fix your hearing aid, honey . . . close . . . tea. My view. See, she *wants* to come. Steady now, that's how." Adding mysteriously: "Remember your advice, easy to keep your head above water, empty things float. Float."

The singing a fading march for them, tall woman with a swollen leg, weaving little man, and the swollen thinness they help between.

The stench in the hall: mildew? decay? "We sit and rest then climb. My gorgeous view. We help each other and here we are."

The stench along into the slab of room. A washstand for a sink, a box with oilcloth tacked around for a cupboard, a three-burner gas plate. Artificial flowers, colorless with dust. Everywhere pictures foaming: wedding, baby, party, vacation, graduation, family pictures. From the narrow couch under a slit of window, sure enough the view: lurching rooftops and a scallop of ocean heaving, preening, twitching under the moon.

"While the water heats. Excuse me . . . down the hall." Ellen Mays has gone.

"You'll live?" he asks mechanically, sat down to feel his fright; tried to pull her alongside.

She pushed him away. "For air," she said; stood clinging to the dresser. Then, in a terrible voice:

After a lifetime of room. Of many rooms.

Shhh.

You remember how she lived. Eight children. And now one room like a coffin.

She pays rent!

Shrinking the life of her into one room like a coffin Rooms and rooms like this I lie on the quilt and hear them talk

Please, Mrs. Orator-without-Breath.

Once you went for coffee I walked I saw A Balzac a Chekhov to write it Rummage Alone On scraps

Better old here than in the old country!

On scraps Yet they sang like like Wondrous! *Humankind* *one has to believe* So strong for what? To rot not grow?

Your poor lungs beg you. They sob between each word.

Singing. Unused the life in them. She in this poor
room with her pictures Max You The children Everywhere unused the life And who has meaning? Century after
century still all in us not to grow?

Coffins, rummage, plants: sick woman. Oh lay down. We will
get for you the doctor.

"And when will it end. Oh, *the end.*" *That* nightmare thought,
and this time she writhed, crumpled against him, seized his hand
(for a moment again the weight, the soft distant roaring of humanity) and on the strangled-for breath, begged: "Man . . . we'll destroy
ourselves?"

And looking for answer—in the helpless pity and fear for her
(for *her*) that distorted his face—she understood the last months,
and knew that she was dying.

4

"Let us go home," she said after several days.

"You are in training for a cross-country run? That is why you do
not even walk across the room? Here, like a prescription Phil said,
till you are stronger from the operation. You want to break doctor's
orders?"

She saw the fiction was necessary to him, was silent; then: "At
home I will get better. If the doctor here says?"

"And winter? And the visits to Lennie and to Clara? All right," for
he saw the tears in her eyes, "I will write Phil, and talk to the doctor."

Days passed. He reported nothing. Jeannie came and took her
out for air, past the boarded concessions, the hooded and tented
amusement rides, to the end of the pier. They watched the spent
waves feeding the new, the gulls in the clouded sky; even up where
they sat, the wind-blown sand stung.

She did not ask to go down the crooked steps to the sea.

Back in her bed, while he was gone to the store, she said: "Jeannie, this doctor, he is not one I can ask questions. Ask him for me, can I go home?"

Jeannie looked at her, said quickly: "Of course, poor Granny. You want your own things around you, don't you? I'll call him tonight. . . . Look, I've something to show you," and from her purse unwrapped a large cookie, intricately shaped like a little girl. "Look at the curls— can you hear me well, Granny?—and the darling eyelashes. I just came from a house where they were baking them."

"The dimples, there in the knees," she marveled, holding it to the better light, turning, studying, "like art. Each singly they cut, or a mold?"

"Singly," said Jeannie, "and if it is a child only the mother can make them. Oh Granny, it's the likeness of a real little girl who died yesterday—Rosita. She was three years old. *Pan del Muerto*, the Bread of the Dead. It was the custom in the part of Mexico they came from."

Still she turned and inspected. "Look, the hollow in the throat, the little cross necklace. . . . I think for the mother it is a good thing to be busy with such bread. You know the family?"

Jeannie nodded. "On my rounds. I nursed. . . . Oh Granny, it is like a party; they play songs she liked to dance to. The coffin is lined with pink velvet and she wears a white dress. There are candles. . . ."

"In the house?" Surprised, "They keep her in the house?"

"Yes," said Jeannie, "and it is against the health law. The father said it will be sad to bury her in this country; in Oaxaca they have a feast night with candles each year; everyone picnics on the graves of those they loved until dawn."

"Yes, Jeannie, the living must comfort themselves." And closed her eyes.

"You want to sleep, Granny?"

"Yes, tired from the pleasure of you. I may keep the Rosita? There stand it, on the dresser, where I can see; something of my own around me."

In the kitchenette, helping her grandfather unpack the groceries, Jeannie said in her light voice:

"I'm resigning my job, Grandaddy."

"Ah, the lucky young man. Which one is he?"

"Too late. You're spoken for." She made a pyramid of cans, unstacked, and built again.

"Something is wrong with the job?"

"With me. I can't be"—she searched for the word—"What they call professional enough. I let myself feel things. And tomorrow I have to report a family. . . ." The cans clicked again. "It's not that, either. I just don't know what I want to do, maybe go back to school, maybe go to art school. I thought if you went to San Francisco I'd come along and talk it over with Momma and Daddy. But I don't see how you can go. She wants to go home. She asked me to ask the doctor."

The doctor told her himself. "Next week you may travel, when you are a little stronger." But next week there was the fever of an infection, and by the time that was over, she could not leave the bed—a rented hospital bed that stood beside the double bed he slept in alone now.

Outwardly the days repeated themselves. Every other afternoon and evening he went out to his newfound cronies, to talk and play cards. Twice a week, Mrs. Mays came. And the rest of the time, Jeannie was there.

By the sickbed stood Jeannie's FM radio. Often into the room the shapes of music came. She would lie curled on her side, her knees drawn up, intense in listening (Jeannie sketched her so, coiled, convoluted like an ear), then thresh her hand out and abruptly snap the radio mute—still to lie in her attitude of listening, concealing tears.

Once Jeannie brought in a young Marine to visit, a friend from high-school days she had found wandering near the empty pier. Because Jeannie asked him to, gravely, without self-consciousness, he sat himself cross-legged on the floor and performed for them a dance of his native Samoa.

Long after they left, a tiny thrumming sound could be heard where, in her bed, she strove to repeat the beckon, flight, surrender of his hands, the fluttering footbeats, and his low plaintive calls.

Hannah and Phil sent flowers. To deepen her pleasure, he placed one in her hair. "Like a girl," he said, and brought the hand mirror so she could see. She looked at the pulsing red flower, the yellow skull face; a desolate, excited laugh shuddered from her, and she pushed the mirror away—but let the flower burn.

The week Lennie and Helen came, the fever returned. With it the excited laugh, and incessant words. She, who in her life had spoken but seldom and then only when necessary (never having learned the easy, social uses of words), now in dying, spoke incessantly.

In a half-whisper: "Like Lisa she is, your Jeannie. Have I told you of Lisa who taught me to read? Of the highborn she was, but noble in herself. I was sixteen; they beat me; my father beat me so I would not go to her. It was forbidden, she was a Tolstoyan. At night, past dogs that howled, terrible dogs, my son, in the snows of winter to the road, I to ride in her carriage like a lady, to books. To her, life was holy, knowledge was holy, and she taught me to read. They hung her. Everything that happens one must try to understand why. She killed one who betrayed many. Because of betrayal, betrayed all she lived and believed. In one minute she killed, before my eyes (there is so much blood in a human being, my son), in prison with me. All that happens, one must try to understand.

"The name?" Her lips would work. "The name that was their pole star; the doors of the death houses fixed to open on it; I read of it my year of penal servitude. Thuban!" very excited, "Thuban, in ancient Egypt the pole star. Can you see, look out to see it, Jeannie, if it swings around *our* pole star that seems to *us* not to move.

"Yes, Jeannie, at your age my mother and grandmother had already buried children . . . yes, Jeannie, it is more than oceans between

88

Olshana and you . . . yes, Jeannie, they danced, and for all the bodies they had they might as well be chickens, and indeed, they scratched and flapped their arms and hopped.

"And Andrei Yefimitch, who for twenty years had never known of it and never wanted to know, said as if he wanted to cry: but why my dear friend this malicious laughter?" Telling to herself half-memorized phrases from her few books. "Pain I answer with tears and cries, baseness with indignation, meanness with repulsion . . . for life may be hated or wearied of, but never despised."

Delirious: "Tell me, my neighbor, Mrs. Mays, the pictures never lived, but what of the flowers? Tell them who ask: no rabbis, no ministers, no priests, no speeches, no ceremonies: ah, false—let the living comfort themselves. Tell Sammy's boy, he who flies, tell him to go to Stuttgart and see where Davy has no grave. And what? . . . And what? where millions have no graves—save air."

In delirium or not, wanting the radio on; not seeming to listen, the words still jetting, wanting the music on. Once, silencing it abruptly as of old, she began to cry, unconcealed tears this time. "You have pain, Granny?" Jeannie asked.

"The music," she said, "still it is there and we do not hear; knocks, and our poor human ears too weak. What else, what else we do not hear?"

Once she knocked his hand aside as he gave her a pill, swept the bottles from her bedside table: "no pills, let me feel what I feel," and laughed as on his hands and knees he groped to pick them up.

Nighttimes her hand reached across the bed to hold his.

A constant retching began. Her breath was too faint for sustained speech now, but still the lips moved:

When no longer necessary   to injure others
Pick   pick pick   Blind chicken
As a human being   responsibility

"David!" imperious, "Basin!" and she would vomit, rinse her

mouth, the wasted throat working to swallow, and begin the chant again.

She will be better off in the hospital now, the doctor said.

He sent the telegrams to the children, was packing her suitcase, when her hoarse voice startled. She had roused, was pulling herself to sitting.

"Where now?" she asked. "Where now do you drag me?"

"You do not even have to have a baby to go this time," he soothed, looking for the brush to pack. "Remember, after Davy you told me—worthy to have a baby for the pleasure of the ten-day rest in the hospital?"

"Where now? Not home yet?" Her voice mourned. "Where *is* my home?"

He rose to ease her back. "The doctor, the hospital," he started to explain, but deftly, like a snake, she had slithered out of bed and stood swaying, propped behind the night table.

"Coward," she hissed, "runner."

"You stand," he said senselessly.

"To take me there and run. Afraid of a little vomit."

He reached her as she fell. She struggled against him, half slipped from his arms, pulled herself up again.

"Weakling," she taunted, "to leave me there and run. Betrayer. All your life you have run."

He sobbed, telling Jeannie. "A Marilyn Monroe to run for her virtue. Fifty-nine pounds she weighs, the doctor said, and she beats at me like a Dempsey. Betrayer, she cries, and I running like a dog when she calls; day and night, running to her, her vomit, the bedpan. . . ."

"She needs you, Grandaddy," said Jeannie. "Isn't that what they call love? I'll see if she sleeps, and if she does, poor worn-out darling, we'll have a party, you and I: I brought us rum babas."

They did not move her. By her bed now stood the tall hooked pillar that held the solutions—blood and dextrose—to feed her veins. Jeannie moved down the hall to take over the sickroom, her face so radiant, her grandfather asked her once: "you are in love?" (Shameful the joy, the pure overwhelming joy from being with her grandmother; the peace, the serenity that breathed.) "My darling escape," she answered incoherently, "my darling Granny"—as if that explained.

Now one by one the children came, those that were able. Hannah, Paul, Sammy. Too late to ask: and what did you learn with your living, Mother, and what do we need to know?

Clara, the eldest, clenched:

Pay me back, Mother, pay me back for all you took from me. Those others you crowded into your heart. The hands I needed to be for you, the heaviness, the responsibility.

Is this she? Noises the dying make, the crablike hands crawling over the covers. The ethereal singing.

She hears that music, that singing from childhood; forgotten sound—not heard since, since. . . . And the hardness breaks like a cry: Where did we lose each other, first mother, singing mother?

Annulled: the quarrels, the gibing, the harshness between; the fall into silence and the withdrawal.

I do not know you, Mother. Mother, I never knew you.

Lennie, suffering not alone for her who was dying, but for that in her which never lived (for that which in him might never come to live). From him too, unspoken words: *good-bye Mother who taught me to mother myself.*

Not Vivi, who must stay with her children; not Davy, but he is already here, having to die again with *her* this time, for the living take their dead with them when they die.

Light she grew, like a bird, and, like a bird, sound bubbled in her throat while the body fluttered in agony. Night and day, asleep or awake (though indeed there was no difference now) the songs and the phrases leaping.

And he, who had once dreaded a long dying (from fear of himself, from horror of the dwindling money) now desired her quick death profoundly, for *her* sake. He no longer went out, except when Jeannie forced him; no longer laughed, except when, in the bright kitchenette, Jeannie coaxed his laughter (and she, who seemed to hear nothing else, would laugh too, conspiratorial wisps of laughter).

Light, like a bird, the fluttering body, the little claw hands, the beaked shadow on her face; and the throat, bubbling, straining.

He tried not to listen, as he tried not to look on the face in which only the forehead remained familiar, but trapped with her the long nights in that little room, the sounds worked themselves into his consciousness, with their punctuation of death swallows, whimpers, gurglings.

Even in reality (swallow) *life's lack of it*

Slaveships   deathtrains   clubs   eeenough

The bell   summon what enables

78,000 in one minute (whisper of a scream) *78,000 human beings   we'll destroy ourselves?*

"Aah, Mrs. Miserable," he said, as if she could hear, "all your life working, and now in bed you lie, servants to tend, you do not even need to call to be tended, and still you work. Such hard work it is to die? Such hard work?"

The body threshed, her hand clung in his. A melody, ghost-thin, hovered on her lips, and like a guilty ghost, the vision of her bent in listening to it, silencing the record instantly he was near. Now, heedless of his presence, she floated the melody on and on.

"Hid it from me," he complained, "how many times you listened to remember it so?" And tried to think when she had first played it, or first begun to silence her few records when he came near—but could reconstruct nothing. There was only this room with its tall hooked pillar and its swarm of sounds.

No man one   except through others
Strong   with the not yet   in the now
Dogma dead   war dead   one country

"It helps, Mrs. Philosopher, words from books? It helps?" And it seemed to him that for seventy years she had hidden a tape recorder, infinitely microscopic, within her, that it had coiled infinite mile on mile, trapping every song, every melody, every word read, heard, and spoken—and that maliciously she was playing back only what said nothing of him, of the children, of their intimate life together.

"Left us indeed, Mrs. Babbler," he reproached, "you who called others babbler and cunningly saved your words. A lifetime you tended and loved, and now not a word of us, for us. Left us indeed? Left me."

And he took out his solitaire deck, shuffled the cards loudly, slapped them down.

Lift high banner of reason (tatter of an orator's voice) *justice   freedom   light*
Humankind   life worthy   capacities
Seeks (blur of shudder) *belong   human being*

"Words, words," he accused, "and what human beings did *you* seek around you, Mrs. Live Alone, and what humankind think worthy?"

Though even as he spoke, he remembered she had not always been isolated, had not always wanted to be alone (as he knew there had been a voice before this gossamer one; before the hoarse voice that broke from silence to lash, make incidents, shame him—a girl's voice of eloquence that spoke their holiest dreams). But again he could reconstruct, image, nothing of what had been before, or when, or how, it had changed.

Ace, queen, jack. The pillar shadow fell, so, in two tracks; in the mirror depths glistened a moonlike blob, the empty solution bottle. And it worked in him: *of reason and justice and freedom . . . Dogma dead*: he remembered the full quotation, laughed bitterly. "Hah, good you do not know what you say; good Victor Hugo died and did not see it, his twentieth century."

Deuce, ten, five. Dauntlessly she began a song of their youth of belief:

These things shall be, a loftier race
than e'er the world hath known shall rise
with flame of freedom in their souls
and light of knowledge in their eyes

King, four, jack "In the twentieth century, hah!"

They shall be gentle, brave and strong
to spill no drop of blood, but dare
all . . .
*   on earth and fire and sea and air*

"To spill no drop of blood, hah! So, cadaver, and you too, cadaver Hugo, 'in the twentieth century ignorance will be dead, dogma will be dead, war will be dead, and for all mankind one country—of fulfillment?' Hah!"

And every life (long strangling cough) *shall*
*   be a song*

The cards fell from his fingers. Without warning, the bereavement and betrayal he had sheltered—compounded through the years—hidden even from himself—revealed itself,

uncoiled,

released,

sprung

and with it the monstrous shapes of what had actually happened in the century.

A ravening hunger or thirst seized him. He groped into the kitchenette, switched on all three lights, piled a tray—"you have finished your night snack, Mrs. Cadaver, now I will have mine." And he was shocked at the tears that splashed on the tray.

"Salt tears. For free. I forgot to shake on salt?"

Whispered: "Lost, how much I lost."

Escaped to the grandchildren whose childhoods were childish, who had never hungered, who lived unravaged by disease in warm houses of many rooms, had all the school for which they cared, could walk on any street, stood a head taller than their grandparents, towered above—beautiful skins, straight backs, clear straightforward eyes. "Yes, you in Olshana," he said to the town of sixty years ago, "they would be nobility to you."

And was this not the dream then, come true in ways undreamed? he asked.

And are there no other children in the world? he answered, as if in her harsh voice.

And the flame of freedom, the light of knowledge?

And the drop, to spill no drop of blood?

And he thought that at six Jeannie would get up and it would be his turn to go to her room and sleep, that he could press the buzzer and she would come now; that in the afternoon Ellen Mays was coming, and this time they would play cards and he could marvel at how rouge can stand half an inch on the cheek; that in the evening the doctor would come, and he could beg him to be merciful, to stop the feeding solutions, to let her die.

To let her die, and with her their youth of belief out of which her bright, betrayed words foamed; stained words, that on her working lips came stainless.

Hours yet before Jeannie's turn. He could press the buzzer and wake her to come now; he could take a pill, and with it sleep; he could pour more brandy into his milk glass, though what he had poured was not yet touched.

Instead he went back, checked her pulse, gently tended with his knotty fingers as Jeannie had taught.

She was whimpering; her hand crawled across the covers for his. Compassionately he enfolded it, and with his free hand gathered up the cards again. Still was there thirst or hunger ravening in him.

That world of their youth—dark, ignorant, terrible with hate and disease—how was it that living in it, in the midst of corruption, filth, treachery, degradation, they had not mistrusted man nor themselves; had believed so beautifully, so . . . falsely?

"Aaah, children," he said out loud, "how we believed, how we belonged." And he yearned to package for each of the children, the grandchildren, for everyone, *that joyous certainty, that sense of mattering, of moving and being moved, of being one and indivisible with the great of the past, with all that freed, ennobled.* Package it, stand on corners, in front of stadiums and on crowded beaches, knock on doors, give it as a fabled gift.

"And why not in cereal boxes, in soap packages?" he mocked himself. "Aah. You have taken my senses, cadaver."

Words foamed, died unsounded. Her body writhed; she made kissing motions with her mouth. (Her lips moving as she read, pouring over the Book of the Martyrs, the magnifying glass superimposed over the heavy eyeglasses.) *Still she believed?* "Eva!" he whispered. "Still you believed? You lived by it? These Things Shall Be?"

"One pound soup meat," she answered distinctly, "one soup bone."

"My ears heard you. Ellen Mays was witness: 'Humankind . . . one has to believe.'" Imploringly: "Eva!"

"Bread, day-old." She was mumbling. "Please, in a wooden box . . . for kindling. The thread, hah, the thread breaks. Cheap thread"— and a gurgling, enormously loud, began in her throat.

"I ask for stone; she gives me bread—day-old." He pulled his hand away, shouted: "Who wanted questions? Everything you have to wake?" Then dully, "Ah, let me help you turn, poor creature."

Words jumbled, cleared. In a voice of crowded terror:

"Paul, Sammy, don't fight.

"Hannah, have I ten hands?

"How can I give it, Clara, how can I give it if I don't have?"

"You lie," he said sturdily, "there was joy too." Bitterly: "Ah how cheap you speak of us at the last."

As if to rebuke him, as if her voice had no relationship with her flailing body, she sang clearly, beautifully, a school song the children had taught her when they were little; begged:

"Not look   my hair   where they cut. . . ."

(The crown of braids shorn.) And instantly he left the mute old woman poring over the Book of the Martyrs; went past the mother treading at the sewing machine, singing with the children; past the girl in her wrinkled prison dress, hiding her hair with scarred hands, lifting to him her awkward, shamed, imploring eyes of love; and took her in his arms, dear, personal, fleshed, in all the heavy passion he had loved to rouse from her.

"Eva!"

Her little claw hand beat the covers. How much, how much can a man stand? He took up the cards, put them down, circled the beds, walked to the dresser, opened, shut drawers, brushed his hair, moved his hand bit by bit over the mirror to see what of the reflection he could blot out with each move, and felt that at any moment he would die of what was unendurable. Went to press the buzzer to wake Jeannie, looked down, saw on Jeannie's sketch pad the hospital bed, with *her*; the double bed alongside, with him; the tall pillar feeding into her veins, and their hands, his and hers, clasped, feeding each other. And as if he had been instructed he went to his bed, lay down, holding the sketch (as if it could shield against the monstrous shapes of loss, of betrayal, of death) and with his free hand took hers back into his.

So Jeannie found them in the morning.

That last day the agony was perpetual. Time after time it lifted her almost off the bed, so they had to fight to hold her down. He could not endure and left the room; wept as if there never would be tears enough.

Jeannie came to comfort him. In her light voice she said: Grandaddy, Grandaddy don't cry. She is not there, she promised me.

97

On the last day, she said she would go back to when she first heard music, a little girl on the road of the village where she was born. She promised me. It is a wedding and they dance, while the flutes so joyous and vibrant tremble in the air. Leave her there, Grandaddy, it is all right. She promised me. Come back, come back and help her poor body to die.

For two of that generation
Seevya and Genya
Infinite, dauntless, incorruptible

Death deepens the wonder

REQUA I

It seemed he had had to hold up his head forever. All he wanted was to lie down. Maybe his uncle would let him, there in that strip of pale sun by the redwoods, where he might get warm.

I got those sittin kinks, too, his uncle said, but you don't see *me* staggerin round like an old drunk . . . Here, shake a leg and let's get wood for a fire. Dry pieces if there is any such. I'll catch the fish.

But he had to heave. Again.

How can you have 'ary a shred left to bring up. Remind me not to take you noplace but by streetcar after this . . . Alright, stretch out; you'll see you're feeling better.

Everything slid, moved, as if he were still in the truck. He had been holding up his head forever. The spongy ground squished under him, and the wet of winter and spring rains felt through the tarp. He was lying on the ground, *the ground*. There might be snakes. The trees stretched up and up so you couldn't see if they had tops, and up there they leaned as if they were going to fall. There hadn't even been time to say good-bye to the lamppost that he could hug and swing himself round and round. Round and round like his head, having to hold it up forever. Being places he had never been. Waiting moving sliding trying. Staying up to take care of his mother, afraid to lie down even if she was quiet, 'cause he might fall asleep and not hear her if she needed him.

Even the sun was cold. Wes took off his mackinaw and threw it over to him. He squinched himself together to try and fit under it. Moving sliding The road was never straight, the pickup bumped and bumped and he had to hold up his head. Even when he threw up, his uncle wouldn't stop. Maybe it was the whiskey they'd had when they got back from that place, made him sick. Or the up all night, up-down sorting and packing, throwing away and loading. Then that wet hoohoo wind on the auto ferry, and the night so dark he didn't even get to see the new bridge they were building.

The trees *were* red, like blood that oozed out of old meat and nobody washed the plate. Under them waved—ferns? Baddream giant ones to the baby kind they put around flowers for too sick people.

He had been holding up his head forever. The creek was slipping and sliding too. His uncle came from nowhere and put three fishes too close to him on a rock. They flopped and moved their sides, trying hard to breathe like too sick people.

He pulled the tarp farther down to the next stripe of sun. A wind made the skinny fire cough gallons of smoke and him shiver even more. Curling and curling till he got all in a ball under the mackinaw and didn't have to see

or smell.

When he woke up, he was warm. Fog curled high between the trees, the light shone rosy soft like a bedroom lamp lit somewhere. By the fire, a harmonica in his hand, his uncle was sleeping. Across the creek, just like in the movie show or in a dream, a deer and two baby deers were drinking. When he lifted his head, they lifted theirs.

For a long time he and the doe looked into each others eyes. Then swift, beautiful, they were gone—but her eyes kept looking into his.

Wes was mad to have conked out like that. Six more hours to go—that's if this heap holds up and we don't get stuck 'hind a load going up a grade. I'll have to put out at work like always tomorrow, and it's sure not any restin we been doin these gone days.

Just like before, but colder. Moving   sliding. Having to hold up his head. Bumproad twisty in a dark moving tunnel of trees. The lumber trucks screamed coming round the bends, and after it was dark their lights made the moving fog look scary. Sometimes he could sleep, sagged against his uncle who didn't move away. Cold or jolts would wake him. He didn't understand how it was that he was sitting up or why he didn't have a bed to lie down in or why or where he was going. All he wanted was to lie down

forever

───────────

A long bridge with standing stone bears. His uncle said: Klamath, almost there. (*Underneath in the night, yearling salmon slipped through their last fresh waters, making it easy to the salt ocean years.*) When the car stopped, there wasn't even a light to see by. A lady came out to help; the light from the open door made the dark stand taller than even the redwoods and *that* leaned like it might fall on him too. The wind or something blew away her words and his uncle's words. His feet were pins and needles   too many boxes and bundles   too many trips down and back a long hall like a cave. A feather cape or something hanging got knocked down. His head gasped back and forth like the sides of the fish on the rock   Something about: we didn't throw away nothin   well I'm sure not goin to miss where I've been   hot milk or coffee?   but he didn't answer, just lay down on a cot with the bundles stacked around him and went into a dream.

So he came to Requa   March, 1932   13 years old.

He stands with his back clamped hard against the door Wes has left open, and he has jumped up from the cot to close.

Hey. Leave it open. My can's still draggin. A block behind.

(*No smile. Skinny little shrimp. Clutching at the door knob, knuckles white, nostrils flaring. Funny animal noises in his throat.*)

Sleeping—all day? Cmon, you had to at least take a leak and put something into that belly . . . Mrs. Ed or Yee didn't stick their nose in? You didn't see nobody? . . . Well (looking around), one thing, you sure weren't neating up the place.

(*Pale. Ol ghostboy. Silent Cal.*) (*Natural—it's plenty raw yet.*)

I been sleepin too—on my feet AND gettin paid for it. That's talent. (*No smile*) I wasn't bawlin you out, we can get squared away tonight or tomorrow . . . Sure you have to come to eat. It'll only be them that stays here. We all get along. You don't bother them, they don't bother you.

They are taking away the boxes and bundles, his low little walls.

That one on top: left over groceries. Into the kitchen, Yee. Forget takin it off the week's board, Mrs. Ed, they didn't cost me nothin. Bedding stuff, Bo; up to the attic. Pots and kitchen things, High. Attic. . . . Well who'd I leave them for and I thought they might be worth a dime or two. Listen, you'd be surprised how many's been in tryin to sell Evans their pots and blankets and everywhich things. Even guns and fishin gear, and thats get-by when nobodys workin. (Lowered voice) Just her clothes, Mrs. Ed, you know anybody? Mrs. Ed's room. Lamps and little rugs, Stevie *said* they was theirs. Sure lay it down, save me a splinter. Looks good. . . . Anyone for a lamp? (Funny noises in the kid's throat.) Gear. *He'll* put 'em away, Mrs. Ed. The bottom drawer, kid, yours and room to spare. Just a mitt? no ball, no bat? . . . Oddsies, endsies. Yah, a radio. Even works:

Kingfish and Madam Queen, here we is. Stevie, Mrs. Edler is talking at you: you got clean stuff for school or does Yee have to wash? No, we never talked is he goin to school or what. . . . I'll tell you this, though, he's not goin through what me and Sis did: kicked round one place after another, not havin nobody. Nobody. Right, Stevie? Can you use a clock, High? Attic. . . . Was you startin to say something, Stevie? (*Ghostboy!* Swallowing, snuffling.) Naw, that last box stays: our ketchall; it'll take time, goin through it.

Wait, Bo, maybe I'll chase along after all   IF you got the do-re-mi. Sattiday night, isn't it? and I feel the week. (*What am I doing, what am I goin to do with this miserable kid?*) Stevie's for the shuteye anyway, aren't you, kid.

Are you for the shuteye, Stevie?

Scratch of a twig on the window. All he has to lull to, who has rocked his nights high on a tree of noise, his traffic city.

Blind thick dark, whose sleep came gentled in streetlamp glow.

And the head on his pillow bulging, though still he is having to hold it up somewhere   And the round and round slipping   sliding   jolting   moved to inside him, so he has to begin to rock his body; rock the cot gently, down and back.

Down and back. It makes a throb for the dark. A clock sound.

That man Highpockets who stuck his hand out at supper and said "Shake, meet the wife" and everybody laughed, he had their clock that stood by the bamboo lamp. A tiny lady in a long dress leaned on it and laughed and held up a tinier flower branch. It had been one of his jobs to wind it and it wheezed while he was winding it.

Jobs.

He couldn't remember, was it Bo had taken the lamp? Telling everybody at the table like it was a joke or important. Would you believe it? He's never been fishin never been huntin never held a gun never been in a boat.

Never   Forever

Down and back. The army blanket itched. When he was a kid he'd really believed that story about they were that color and scratchy because of blood and mud and poo and powdered licy things from the war that never could get washed out

Down and back   A clock sound   It keeps away

What had happened with the bloody quilt? Soft quilt   She hadn't even asked how he was when they let him in after all that waiting and waiting to see her   Just: *did you   soak   my quilt?* Burning eyes

Gentle eyes that looked long at him   blood dripping from where should be eyes   Out in the hall swathed bodies floating like in bad movies   never touching the ground   at the window

down and back   down and back

If he had the lamp   the boxes

You promised   and see I'm someplace else again   dark and things that can get me and I don't know where anything is. Don't expect *me* to be 'sponsible

they should have put the clock and lamp in with her   the boxes and bundles and wall and put them round her   everything would be together   he wouldn't have to try and remember   or hold up his head that wouldn't lay down inside the one on the pillow so he could sleep

down and back   down and back

––––––––––

All that week he would be lying on the cot in the half dark when Wes got home from work; jump up to re-close the door; lie down again until Wes made him wash up, go in to supper.

At the table he looked at no one, answered in monosyllables, or seemed not to hear at all, stared at the wall or at his wrist, messed the food on his plate into the form of one letter or another, hardly ate

Supper over, he would walk somnambule back to the gaunt room, take off his shoes, get under the covers and lie there, one hand over his eyes.

Bo, Hi, crowded in chattering alongside the radio or playing a quick round of cards; Wes oiling his boots for work, tinkering with fishing-hunting gear, playing the harmonica; or the room empty: lying there, his arm over his eyes snuffling   scratching   swallowing

One Monday (let him be a while, Mrs. Ed had said), Wes, on his way to work, left the boy at the Klamath crossroads to wait the school bus.

He stands motionless in the moist fog that is almost rain, in Bo's too big fishing slicker. Blurs of shapes loom up and pass. Once a bindle stiff plods by. The across-the-road is blotted out.

When the bus stops and the door snorts open, he still does not move. The driver tries three honks, pokes his head out and yells: c'mon New, whatever your name, I'm late. You can do your snoozing inside.

Laughter from in the bus. In hoots.

Slowly, as if returning from an infinite distance, the boy focusses his eyes on the driver, shaking his head and moving his lips as if speaking. He is still mutely shaking "No," as the faces at the grimy windows begin to slip by   fast and faster   contorted or vacant or staring.

On *his* face, lifted to the fog, is duplicated one by one, the expressions on the faces of his fellow young. Still he stands, his lips moving. When he has counted thirteen cars passing (a long while), he crosses and goes back down the road, the way his uncle had brought him.

———

Days.

This time when Wes got home, his neatly made bed was torn up, its blanket bunched round the boy stretched out in dimness near the window.

At the expected convulsive jumpup, Wes stepped back and grabbed the doorknob himself. Alright, alright, I'm closing it. The law ain't chasin *me*. Are they chasin you?

(but the boy had not moved at all)

He felt like yelling: why do you do that   or: look at me for once, say hello.

Instead he sat down heavily in the big chair, unlaced his boots. No, I won't ask what he's been doin. Nothin. He'll say it in nothin, too.

Night scratched at the window and seeped from the room corners. No other sound but rising river wind.

The work of the day (of the week, of years) slumped onto Wes. For a minute he let go, slept: snored, great sobbing snores. In a spasm of effort, jerked awake, regarded the shadows, the rumple on the floor by the window.

Something about the light, the radio, not being snapped on; the absence of the usual attempted pleasantries; some rhythm not right, roused the boy from the trancing secret tremble of leaves against the low glowing sky. Was that his mother or his uncle sagged there in the weight of weariness, and why were her feet on the floor?

Get back   he said implacably   Your footstool's gone too   In a box or throwed away or somebody else resting their tootsies on it   Serves you right   How you going to put up your feet and rub on the varicose like you like to, now?

(*Blue swollen veining*) (*Are you tired, Ma? Tired to death, love.*)

What are you twitchin your muscles like a flybit horse for? asked Wes. And stop swallowin snot.

He slept again   This man he hardly knew who came and took everything and him and put him in another place he did not know where he was. Slumped, sagged, like . . .

Wes, if you set your feet up on something. *WES*

If I what?

If you set your feet up on a box

A box. For Crizake

Or a chair   and rub where your feet hurt
A box   Say, did you do up that box today like I told you?
It rests them, Wes. You rub up, not down
Answer me. Did you? No. You leave the only thing I ask you
to do, for me to do, on my day off   My one day   Just look at this
place   You didn't help High neither when I asked you   You think
the candlefish run is goin to last forever? Maybe you might of brung
in a basket or two   Mrs. Ed would've took it into consideration   You
cost boy   ghostboy   don't you know that? My Saturday night for
one thing   my one night to howl   you're costin

(Shrimp!) (I'd better watch it; I'm really spoiling tonight.) A rancor-
ous: What's goin to be with you, you dummy kid? raps out anyway.

Sounding a long plaintive mockcowboy howl, switching on the
light, yanking him up (God, he's skinny) and with a shove that is
half embrace, steers the kid in to dinner.

Where he'd pushed the boiled salt salmon and potatoes away, the
crack on his plate said: *Y. You cost, boy, you cost.* In his wrist a little
living ball pushed, as if trying to get out   Where the visiting nurse
put her pinky and counted   too sick people

Sagged with weariness   like Wes   her stockings rolled down
rubbing   rubbing   where the blue veins swoll

On the wall the bottom of the Indian bow made: *U.* No, a funny
V. Y. V. Vaud-e-ville. He'd stay for it twice and the feature twice and
maybe the serial too   while the light the silvery light   Face bigger and bigger on the screen   Closer   Vast glutinous face   Sour
breath   *IS YOU DERE, CHARLIE?*

Bo. Only Bo. Everybody at the table laughing

And now the faces start up   bigger than the room   on the fast
track   Having to hold up   Hurry

At the door, Wes heard it again, that faint rhythmic creak. The
first time, nights ago, he had thought: is the little bastard jacking

off? but it wasn't that kind of a sound. Switching the light on, he saw the boy—as usual—lying on the cot, arm over his face—yes, and rolled into *his* blanket. The sound had stopped.

Sit up. Don't you know enough to excuse yourself when you leave a table sudden? Mrs. Edler was askin me, could you go upriver with her tomorrow to the deer or jumpdance or some such Indian thing they're having up at Terwer. She must want white company bad.

Is you dere, Charlie? You jumped a mile when Bo yelled that into your mug. Serves you right, sitting there night after night like you're no place at all, hardly answerin if people talk to you. Why are you such a snot? *Why?* (*savagely*) IS YOU DERE?

(*Somewhere.*

But the stupor, the lostness, the torpor) (*the safety*)
Keep away you rememorings slippings slidings having to
hold up my head Keep away you trying to get me's
Become the line on a plate, on a wall The rocking and the
making warm the movement of leaves against sky
I work so hard for this safety Let me a while Let me)

—C'mon. Set up like you belong. We're going to get shed of that box. Right now. But first you make up my bed. Just *keep* that blanket you dragged round the floor, and give me yours.

—C'mon, tuck those corners in. We keep things neat around here. Monday you're starting school. For sure this time. No more of this laying round.

—Neat, I said. Now, where's that goddamn box. And quit making those damn noises.

Scooping onto the bed:

boy-sitting-on-a-chamber-pot ash tray Happy Joss Hollywood California painted fringed pillow cover kewpie doll green glass vase, cracked

Jesus, what junk

tiny India brass slipper ash tray enamel cigarette case, Fujiyama scene (thrown too close to the edge of the bed, it

slithers off, slips down behind)   pencils, rubber banded
Junk is right. We sure throwed it in in a hurry
   Plush candy box: sewing stuff: patches   buttons in
   jars   stork scissors   pincushion doll, taffeta bell skirt
   glistening with glass pinheads
Now you got a dolly to play with   Ketch   Can't you even ketch?
   Red plush valentine box: nestled in the compartments:
   brown baby hair, ribbon tied   perfume bottle, empty   china
   deer miniature, the fawn headless   heart locket, stone missing   sand dollar   gull feather
close quick

Now why did we . . .
   tarnished mesh purse: in it a bright penny   lipstick
   rouge-powder compact, slivered mirror   powder sifts
close quick

Pictures:
   palm size, heart shaped fame
onto the bureau

   celluloid frame, tin laddered back stand
onto the bureau

   stained oblong cardboard, smaller snapshots clipped round
   the large center one (His hand falters, steadies)
onto the bureau

   More boxes, slender, rubber banded: in the first: letters
   tied in a man's handkerchief   tin collar button red garter
   band   ribboned medal pinned to a yellow envelope   In
   the second: (vicious the rubber band snaps)
DON'T

The boy rigid on the floor, eyes glazed, mouth open, fixed; face
contorted. A fit?
   Steve? Stevie?
   Crawling now, a snake. Rising. With the pillow batting the box
out of Wes's hands, flailing at him. *Put it back.* With the pillow

shoving everything off the bed into the box. *Put it back. If you was dead   you'd put it back*   With the pillow pushing the box into the hall   slamming the door   *all of it   dead   bury   buried*   Runs to the chamberpot   vomits   jabs at Wes when he tries to help   Runs to the door to run out   sees the box   runs back   takes the coverlet to him and rocks

Alright   alright   Easy   Some other day   where was my marbles? Phew   Just a bad day, Stevie   mine was a Lulu   Alright, it's over   It was too soon, I know   All her things   Alright   Easy

Heaving again.

You through? I'll get it out of here. (Almost falling over the box on his way to empty the slop.) (No, nobody home I can bum a drink off of. Sattiday night . . .) (*What am I doing   what am I going to do with this miserable kid?*)

Bawling now like a girl.

Alright! It's over, Stevie   It got me too   Easy   You got to grab hold . . . It's no good for you, all this layin round   never goin out like normal   Monday you'll start school   Keep you busy   You'll be with other kids, play ball, have somebody to fish with   Not lay around all the time   thinkin about her, feelin bad.

Stopping his rocking. I don't. I don't.

Easy. It's all right; it's natural. But now you got to take hold.

Shut up bastard. Jabbing at him. Shut up. I told you I don't think about her, I don't feel bad. She's dead. Don't you know she's dead, don't you know?

Fending him off   nodding wordlessly (*don't I know?*) Edging him back to the cot   Easy   Do I have to paste you one? Forget it, try to sleep, fella   There's just so much I can stand   Easy   I'm so tired I could drop   I'll help you to catch hold, Steve, I promise I'll help   Stop now   Try to sleep   Holding him down to the cot   I'm tryin. Doing the best I can, even if it turns out worse like usual   But tryin. You try too. You hear that, Stevie? You try too.

Having to hold up

The pictures stayed, untouched, face down on the dresser. Wherever the box went, Was assumed it was to the attic. Days later, making his bed, he found the cigarette case, slipped it into a drawer against that far time he might no longer have to roll his own, could afford tailor-mades.

The boy would not rouse. Shaken awake, would not come to breakfast, refused to go out with him and Bo. "We was goin to start you practice shootin today, try for some fish, maybe even let you take the wheel awhile. *You're* the loser." But Wes did not do much urging, wanting to get away from the incomprehensible moil of with-that-boy.

Before he went, he left instructions: Don't lay down *once*, not once. Neat up this room. If there's going to be any hot water, get yourself scrubbed up for school tomorrow   squeak clean. Find out has Yee got some work you can do; God, what in hell CAN you do. Get outside even if it's raining   down to the river   throw rocks or something. Keep yourself moving   Hear? And don't try to con me.

Asleep in the big chair when Wes got back; no, not asleep (hair still wet and an almost phosphorescent shine on his face) (*ghostboy*) So   *gone*, Wes's breath stopped for a moment. Maybe I ought to get a doc, or ask Mrs. Ed to look in the doctor book. But what would she look for?   laying around?   throwin up?   actin nuts?

Then the dazed, shocked eyes looked at him   but the voice said, perfectly normal: I did everything like you told. Yee cooked him and me rice chow yuk so I don't have to go in for supper tonight, do I. How was your fishing, Wes?

He did not go to school.

Clean to his one white shirt with its streaks of blueing, clutching his and Wes's lunch pails, he sat silent in the pickup till Wes slowed for the crossroads stop where, three weeks before, he had been left for the school bus. Quickly he is over the side.

Hey, *I'm* taking you. You forget? WAIT! Where do you think you're heading?

Plodding back towards Requa.

Get back here. Listen, don't pull no girl tantrum. Get in.

Having to pull over to the shoulder, park, run after him. His violent grab missing, so that he tears the sleazy jacket, half yanking down the boy.

I'm not going, Wes.

Get up, you're going all right. If I have to drag you.

I'd leave as soon as you were gone, Wes.

Starting down the road again.

Spinning him around, socking him a good one, steering him back into the car. (*What am I doing, what am I going to do*)

—What you got against school anyway?

—You're headed straight for the nuthouse, layin round like you've been doing. Just nuttier every day. I'm not going to let you.

—I'll have the truant officer, see? Wait, is 14 or 16 the limit?

—You're goin, see. What the hell else you got to do? C'mon, dust yourself off. I can't be late.

Starting to climb out again.

Really hurting him; pinning him back, banging and banging his head against the wheel, against the seat. You *have* to go, see?

Wes (in a strangled voice) Wes   you're hurting. If I find me a job?

A job! Releasing him in disgust. You ARE in a nutworld. Half the grown men in the county's not working, High's down to two days, and this dummy kid talks about a job.

In Frisco then, Wes? Maybe set up pins again. Or ship?

In Frisco, my God. It's worse there, you know that. And how you goin to make that 500 miles? And who you got in your corner there? Nobody. You NEED learnin.

Starting up the motor.

Wes, I'll jump.

Socking him again. Hard.

Wes, if I go with you? Ask Mr. Evans, can I help? A learn job, Wes. By you.

Something in the boys voice . . . This time Wes's hands on his shoulders are gentle. Steve, don't fight it no more. It's five, maybe six weeks to vacation . . . fishin You'll have buddies. Maybe you're even goin to like school. And even if you don't, sometimes in this life you got to do what you *don't* like. (*Sometimes!*) Evans ain't about to put anybody on—if he did, Ez would be first choose; every week Ez is in askin: can he have his job back . . . Evans don't have it, Stevie. Sometimes its slow even for me. And everythings credit or trade-in; when we get a nickel, he bites it, makes sure its real. I'm surprised he pays *me*.

Ask him, Wes. You said: I'll help you, Steve. You said it. He don't have to pay me. You hurt me, Wes. A learn job. By you. You promised.

Not school

Never

Forever

NEW   USED

U NAME IT—WE GOT IT

U ASK IT—WE FIX IT

Gas   Butane   Sportsmens Goods

Auto Parts   Fittings   Tools

Lumber   Rags   Scrap iron

Electric/plumber/builder supply

Housefurnish things

Auto Repair   Towing   Wrecking

Machining   Soddering   Welding

Tool & Saw Sharping

Glass work   Boat caulking/repair

(Leaky, appraising eyes) Sure, why not? Favor to you, Wes. Anything he gets done, we're that much ahead. But if he's in the way, or it don't work out, that's it. And he's *your* headache. Anybody stick their nose in, he's helping you, not working for me. Don't get him expecting anything for the piggy bank, either. Used stock sometime maybe, whatever I think it's worth and he's worth. Catch?

Tumble of buildings and sheds, stockpiles and junk—a block from the bridge—sprawled in the crotch between 101 going north/south and the short crooked upriver road to game and Indian country.

Landscape of thinghillocks and mounds innumerable. Which shed is which? The wind blows so. Too close: scaly, rapid river; too close: dwarfing, encircling: dark massive forest rise.

Stumbling the mounds in his too thin jacket or Bo's too big slicker after Wes. (*got to figure out what's simple enough he can do. Keep him up. Moving. Paying attention.*) Helping haul   drag   break apart; find the right sized used tire   generator   lumbersash; hand the measure   the part   the tool

I said the red devil   Red devil glass cutter   Your ears need reaming?

Does that even *look* like a 16 x 120? Why the thing they throw peanuts at could figger it

What you breathin like that for? I showed you: if you lift it this way she goes easy. Easy. A right way and a wrong way—easy is the right way.

Is that a shimmy or a shiver? I ought to take me a razor cut, see is it blood or icewater runs in your carcass

The mess heap. Your baby to red up when I'm not needin you. Stack everything, that's what's here, everything—with its own kind. If theys a pile or shed already for it, get it over there   Whats too far gone or cant be burnt, leave. Get them rotten carpets   mattresses   out first. Then them batteries   Pile 'em so. Where I expect to spot you when you're not workin with me, see?

Into the tool shed when it rains. Sort outa the bins into these

here washboilers: like, pipe fittins: brass here   copper there: el-
bows   flanges   unions   couplings   bends   tees. Check out the
drawers, see just what belongs is in 'em; get acquainted: like this
row: wing nuts   castellated   slotted   quarter inch   *Pay attention!*
  Heaps   piles   glut   accumulation
   Sores   cuts   blisters on his hands
    Don't look: scaly rapid river   dark forest encircling

Cold   hardly comprehending   wearing out so quick

 Didn't you hear me callin? Answer me. What you staring
at? You paralyzed? (*ghostboy*) Drop that carpet and get out
of sight till you can come to   Do I have to paste you one?
 (The stiff mouldy rug breaks like cardboard in his hands.
 Underneath maggot patterns writhe)
Can't you tell the difference between taper and spiral fluted?
(lock or finish washer?) (adapter, extension?) can't you?
can't you?
Who said you could come in here and lay down? You sure
tire instant   Get yourself back to the burn pile and throw
that filthy ragquilt out of here. No wonder you're always
scratching.
Is that all you got done and I let you alone all mornin for
it? What's there goin to be show Evans you're of use   Yah,
as much use as the tit on a bull   O for Crizake, you're not
here at all

More and more wrapped in the peacock quilt, rocking, scratching,
snuffling. Rain on the tool shed roof; the little kerosene stove hissing
warmth through its pierced crown. Wes looming in the doorway, the
gray face of evening behind him. C'mon, useless. 6:30. You killed
another day. I *knowed* this was never going to work.
 And once, in the most mournful of voices: Can't you do no bet-

ter? I can't stand it, Stevie. You're ending up in the dummy or loony house, for sure.

But the known is reaching to him, stealthily, secretly, reclaiming.
Sharp wind breath, fresh from the sea. Skies that are all seasons in one day. Fog   rain. *Known weather of his former life.*
Disorder twining with order. The discarded, the broken, the torn from the whole: weatherbeaten   weatherbeaten: mouldering, or waiting for use-need. *Broken existences that yet continue.*

    Hasps   switches   screws   plugs   tubings   drills
    Valves   pistons   shears   planes   punchers   sheaves
    Clamps   sprockets   coils   bits   braces   dies

How many shapes and sizes; how various, how cunning in application. Human mastery, human skill. Hard, defined, enduring, they pass through his hands—link to his city life of manmade marvel.

Wes: junking a towed-in car, one hundred pieces out of what had been one. Singing—unconscious, forceful—to match the motor hum as he machines a new edge, rethreads a pipe. Capable, fumbling; exasperated, patient; demanding, easy; uncomprehending, quick; harsh, gentle: *concerned* with him. *The recognizable human bond.*

The habitable known, stealthily, secretly, reclaiming.
The dead things, pulling him into attention, consciousness.
The tasks: coaxing him with trustworthiness, pliancy, doing as
    he bids

                    having to hold up

Rifts:
Wes sets the pitch, the feed, the slide rest to chase a thread.
"Wes, *let* me. We're learning it in shop. It's my turn again Monday."
(Monday! What Monday? A Monday cobweb weeks   miles   gone life ago) Hard, reassuring, the lathe burrs; spins under his hands. (Somewhere in cobweb mist, a school—speck size. Somewhere smaller specks that move   speak   have faces)

Watch it! O my God, you dummy. How'm I going to explain *this* one to Evans.

Wheat wreathes enameled on a breadbox he is tipping to empty of rain   Remembered pattern; forgotten hunger   peanut butter, sour french bread   Remembered face, hand, wavering through his face, reflected in the rusty agitated water.

He lifts the wrecking mallet, pounds. Long after the spurting water has dried from his face and the tin is shreds in great muddy earth gouges, he still mindlessly pounds.

Later, dragging a mattress to the burn pile, his face contorts, fixes rigid, mouth open. The rest of the day in the toolshed, to lie immobile, and will not get up even to Wes's kick of rage.

Rags stiff and damp   Green slime braids with the rope coils, white grubs track his palm
Bottle fly colors lustre the rotting harness   rusty tongueless bells fall

Only the rain saves him—otherwise, before lunch, he practices shooting. Buckets, cans, are spotted in a semicircle for targets, the rococo scroll of a carpet beater nailed to a post. Sight. Squeeze. Splat. Shuddering rock of the recoil.

Who barks more, Wes or the gun? If you'd been concetrating if you'd just been concetrating. I want you good as me, Stevie. See? 200 yards   right on target everytime.

The bruise on his shoulder—from when? Wes's beating the day he would not go to school?—purples, spreads.

Maybe this is better'n school for you Stevie   Keep you outdoors, build you up   I got so much to learn you   All your life you can use it.

He is warmer now. An old melton coat with anchor buttons that Evans let Wes take from the clothes shed. Faint salt of a seaman's many voyagings seems to nest in it, and deep in the pockets, mysterious graininesses crumble. Afternoons, if the strong northwest winds of May have cleared the sky an hour or two, the coat distills, stores the sun about him as he moves through mound-sheltered warmth in and out of the blowing cold; or sits with Wes, poncho over the muddy ground, eating their baloney and bread lunch in the sun-hive the back of the scrapiron pile makes.

Weeds, the yellow wild mustard and rank cow parsnip, are already waist high, blow between him and river. Blue jays shrill, swoop for crumbs; chipmunks hover. Wes gabs, plays his harmonica. The boy lies face down in his pool of warmth. In him something keeps trembling out in the wind with the torn whirled papers, the bending weeds, the high tossed gulls.

Helping at the gas pump, he keeps his head lowered so that he knows the grease spots on the ground and how they change from day to day, but not who is in the cars. Even when the speech comes glottal, incomprehensible, Indian, he will not look up on the faces, nor on those of the riggers and swampers checking the chains tight around the two-three giant logs that make up their load.

Grease spots, and how they change from day to day; loggers muddied boots, flowerets and pine needles embedded; pliant redwood hair strands loosened from the logs and blowing across the road; the cars of the regulars; Evans dry ghost cough from the store, and that a certain worn-to-bareness tire tread will bring him watchfully into hearing distance; these he comes to know—but never faces.

Once, checking tires (young swaggering voices in the car), a girl steps out on the running board, so close he can smell her, round his hand to her bared thigh, the curve of her butt.

Relentless, vehement: clamor congests   engorges. Gas bite, the soaked rag held to his nostrils, will not help.

Wes, don't call me to the pumps any more.

You'll do as you're told, you snotty kid   Snotty's right   Everytime
I look at you.   Wipe that nose.   You need a washer in there?

relentless

engorged

clamorous

stealthily secretly reclaiming

Terrible pumps:

Evans out more and more.

Davis does what *I* say, see? Pay on the line or no tow. You heard
me, no dough, no go. I don't care *how* many kids you got stuck in
your jalopy, or how far you had to hitch to get here. Sure we got a
used transmission. We got a used everything. But for do-re-mi. Don't
ask *me* how you're going to manage without a heap . . . Well, you can
junk it.

No, not even for five gallons trade, I won't take that mattress. I
got a shed full now. There's maybe four hundred families the fifty
miles around; they're sleeping on something already; who's going
to buy 'em off me? No. That spare hasn't got a thousand miles left.
Well maybe the gun.

Ten gallons gets you up—say—Grants Pass. How do *I* know how
you'll make it to your brothers in Chehalis. One thing we *don't* sell
here is a crystal ball.

. . . You'd think it was me knocked up their old ladies and lost
'em their jobs.

Whisper: over here, Wes. I don't want ol Skinflint to spot me.
You think you might have some link chain like this? An /8th or
maybe a quarter inch. I got this idea, see? Sport season coming, and
you know how they like to bring back a souvenir. Well, Christmas

we didn't know what to do, so I whittled the boys up little lumber trucks—load of logs, chain and all—they're still playing with 'em. I thought till the woods open up again, I might pick up some loose change makin 'em to sell. Esty's doing up dolls out of redwood hair. Real cute. Evans won't help me out, but you will, won't you Wes. I'm about out of my mind.

When I call you I don't mean tomorrow sometime next week. If I catch you cuddlin up to that stove again, I'll turn you every which way but loose

———

The smell or the whiskey is making him sick   is making him happy   is making him sleepy   The brights and the ragtime making him happy   lights lights little lights over the fireplace going on and off and on if you wink your eyes in time   I love you lights   Are you howling Wes   is that how you howl   your night to howl? O Wes   in the blue of smoke and breaths tapdancing with Bo and that lady Esty in the middle and that fatso man   Stop   you don't know how to tap, Wes   The keys on the player piano nickel in the slot piano know how   jigging and tapping and nobody's playing them because I'M playing them   long distance   knowing how   tapping and dancing (luxurious round the table   round the dollars   his fingers tapping) round and round

What you going to do with those two big beautiful cartwheels honey? Tapdance my fingers round and round them   what he didn't answer her and should have   because   because   and here the breathblue smokeblue clouded into his head   and on and off and round   tiniest sparkle on the wall   calendar snow scene, moose locking horns   sparkly I love you   O I like that ragtime   kitten on the keys   I *am* the keys   What did you say that's so ha ha Wes? wave wave dance my hand (no nobody's looking) highstep   o highstep and off and on and round   I wanta go to a movie show   and

round   Red light that squiggles to you in the fog and when you get
closer says   E A T   but nobody's eating   they're dancing   they
think its dancing   chewing the rag and swiggling and off and on
and sparkle and round and fire jumping and Wes howling
          Stop that, Bo

                                        sticky and cold, the whiskey
doused over him. *Best hair tonic there is, I'm tellin you, kid, use it myself
every celebratin night   and it stinks so purty*

    It doesn't   it doesn't   and it doesn't wipe off and the smell is
on his sleeve now so when he has to wipe his nose or wave his arm
is making him sick   and off and on   and round   o put another
nickel in   reeling waltz   I wanta go to a picture show   a man
crying (Fatso)   *sobby sentimental stew*   O ma, that's funny, a sobby
sentimental stew
    Liar   You promised   and see I'm another place again   no mov-
ies and no stores and no Chinatown and cold water in the faucet you
have to pump   not even lights   just tonight   little prickle kind
and one squiggle sign   just tonight
    and round and round and off and on   push on the
keys   dance   tap   float on the sadness   sleep pushing down
clouding and   Sure I'm listening Wes   No thanks you just gave
me another nip   Yah   *how you keep Evans from catching on that I'm
not all there*   Yah   and round   sparks like blows from a fist   the
fire?   over the fireplace, branching antlers, sad deer eyes   in the
fire, branching antlers   glowing eyes   am going to be sick
                                        aaagh
                                        aaagh

A dream? The yard   lithe Bo tapdancing the mounds   Wes in the
furnish shed handing out bottles   gurgling from one himself   boot-
leg   he don't know I know he's peddlin hooch but I do, gettin in

on it just when it's goin to get legal   end hard times   Turning
round and round a musical saw wheel   dry whispery papery sad
sound   *they have taken her to Georgia*   Wes's harmonica prowl papery
sad   *there to wear her life away*   making his saddest trainwhistle
sounds   round   and   round

––––––––

The damp rushing air slaps slaps the boys face: *wake up*   the lurching
in his belly, the pitching truck: *wake up* Wes slapping too, jabbing
him away with his elbow every lurch he is thrown against him;
waves of drunk smell from Wes's breath or is it his own sleeve:
wake up. Wes driving jolty, not like Wes at all: shouting   singing   mumbling   beating on the dash. Crooning: poor ol shrimp
cant sit up   poor ol shrimp passin out   Take him out to celebrate
Evans shakin loose two smackers and he cant take it   cant celebrate   FOOderackysacky want some seafood momma shrimpers
and rice are very nice   poor old shrimp (pounding on the dash)
YOU'RE A SHIT EVANS YOU HEAR ME (whispering) he don't
know though does he (elbow jab) he don't know   you're not all there
(loud) cause I cover up good don't I Stevie? We'll have a heaver on
that, hey? Me, not you, shrimp. Am taking care of you like I promised. Right?

   Vamp me honey kitchaleecoo anything you'll want we'll do   Jab.
Forever long to get to Mrs. Eds. Not the same way they came. Jolt,
jolt. Is it even a road? Headless shadows in the carlights. Stumps.
Not all there Sparks like blows Hurtled, falling   falling   Wet
on his face   fir needles   leaves   Blood?

   C'mon, up, up. See if you're hurt. Well I did stop sudden. You're
fine, kid, sound as a dollar. Go ahead, puke. I got to go to this place
down here, see?

   Thick   oblivious   laughing   mumbling   pawing the floor of
the truck for something, throwing the poncho at him, hard   *Cover
up* Don't want you ketching cold. You're running out of snot as is.

Counting, recounting his silver by the light of a flash. Expansively: Keep 'em, Stevie, keep 'em; don't need 'em.

Need what? Thick black   His trembling body redoing the hurtling fall over and over   all scraped places burning. His shoulder . . . Far down in trees a weak light   whorled, spectral, veined   Eyes

Wes, wait, wait for me. Tripping over the poncho. On the ground again, his nose bubbling blood.

Easier to just lie there   roll into the poncho   shrink into the coat   Cry (In one soft pocket his fingers tap round and round the silver dollars; in the other, hold the tongueless bell.) Put another nickel   Some celebrating! *Not all there*

Faint salt smell   from drying blood? the coat? Warm. Round and round   not even minding the dark

Sudden the knowledge where Wes has gone. *Annie Marines*, she sells it. Nausea. Swelling, swollen aching. Helpless, his hand starts to undo the coat layer (*meet the wife, meet the wife*).

Slap. On his face. Another slap. Great drops. *Rain.* Move, you dummy. Pushing himself up against a tree, giant umbrella in the mottled dark. Throb sound in and around him (his own excited blood beat?) Rain, hushing, lapping

City boy, he had only known rain striking hard on unyielding surface, walls, pavement; not this soft murmurous receiving: leaves, trees, earth. In wonder he lay and listened, the fir fragrance sharp through his caked nostrils. Warm. Dry.

Gently he began to rock. The hardness had gone down by itself.

Far down where Wes was, a branch shook silver into the light. Rain. *His mothers quick shiver as the rain traced her cheek. C'mon baby, we've got to run for it.*

Laughing. One of her laughing times. Running fast as her, the bundles bumping his legs. Running up the stairs too. Tickling him, keeping him laughing while she dried his face with the rough towel.

Twisting away from the pain: trying to become the cocoa steam, the cup ring marking the table, the wheat wreathed breadbox. *Her shiver.* How the earth received the rain, how keen its needles. Don't ask *me* where your umbrella got put, don't expect *me* to be sponsible, you in your leaky house.

Rain underneath, swelling to a river, floating her helpless away   *Her shiver*

Twisting away from the pain: face contorted, mouth fallen open: fixed to the look on her dying, dead face.

When Wes lurched down the path, he still did not move. The helpless pain came again. For Wes this time, drunk, stumbling, whispering: O my God, I've had better imagines, O my God.

Stevie! Where the hell are you? You scared the hell out of me . . . Let's get going. I feel lower than whale shit, and that's at the bottom of the ocean.

The light was still on. Wes must have carried or walked him in, been too drunk to make him wake up, undress. Wes hadn't undressed either, lay, shoes muddy on his bed, he, who was always the neat one.

The boy stared at the bulb staring at him; then, painfully, got up, pulled off his clothes, went over and knelt by Wes's bed to tug off the offending shoes and cover him.

One of Wes's fists trembled; a glisten of spit trickled out of the corner of his mouth. His fly was open. How rosy and budlike and quiet it sheathed there.

The blanket ends wouldn't lap to cover. He had to pile on his coat, Wes's mackinaw, and two towels, patting them carefully around the sleeping form. *There now you'll be warm,* he said aloud, *sleep sweet, sweet dreams* (though he did not know he had said it, nor in whose inflections.)

He was shivering with cold now. *Dummy or crazy house   not all there*   Though he put his hands out imploringly to protect himself, the blows struck at him again. His uncle moaned, whispered some-

thing; he leaned down to hear it, looked full on the sleeping face.
Face of his mother. *His* face. Family face.

For once he was glad to turn off the light and have the shutting
darkness: hugged the pillow over his face for more. At the window
spectral shapes tapped; out in the hall, swathed forms floated, wrung
their hands. Later he hurtled the fall over and over in a maggoty sieve
where eyes glowed in rushing underground waters and fire branch
antlers, fir needle after shining needle.

accurately threaded, reamed and chamfered
    Shim   Imperial flared
       cutters   benders   grinders   beaders
          shapers   notchers   splicers   reamers
                       how many shapes and sizes,
                       how various, how cunning in
                             application

What did Toots and Casper want? Did I hear them asking for
two gallons of gas? *Two* gallons? Where they coming from anyway?
I thought that kind were all riding 99.

Tentacle weeds pierce the dishpan he is trying to pry up. Orange
rust flowerings flake, cling to the quivering stalks, embroider the
gaping pan holes.

Beauty of rot   rust   mold

Wingding anchors   bearing sheaves   plated, crackle, mottle
blue, satin finish

Are you dreamin or workin? That carbon should of been clean
chipped off by now. I *promised* that motor. O for Crizake, you ain't
here at all.

Something is different at Mrs. Eds. Is it the longer light? How clear everyone is around the table, though he still does not look into their faces. The lamps, once so bright and hung with shadows, are phantom pale now; the windows, once black mirrors where apparitions swam, show green and clear to heads of trees, river glint, dark waver of hill against sunset sky.

Highpockets is gone. When had he gone, and why? The blurredness will not lift. A new man, thready, pale, sits in his place and has his room.

The talk eddies around him: ain't going to *be* no season, not in Alaska Vancouver or Pedro . . . like crabs feedin on a dead man, like a lot of gulls waitin for scraps . . . the Cascades the Olympics the Blues . . . nickel snatchin bastards

He sees that it is not shadows that hang on the wall around the bow, but Indian things: a feathered headdress, basket hats, shell necklace. Two faces dream in shell frames. One, for all the beard, Mrs. Ed's.

family face

----

sharping   hauling   sorting   splicing
burring   chipping   grinding   cutting
grooving   drilling   caulking   sawing

the tasks, coaxing

rust gardens

Nippers. You bring nippers. Did you think I was going to *bite* the wire? Try it with *your* choppers.

Pilings on pilings. Rockers, victrolas, flyspecked mirrors, scroll trundle sew machines, bureaus, bedsteads, baby buggies.

Wes, I can't hardly open the door, it won't go in, there's no room.

No room, you make room, dummy. That's the job. You good for anything?

The wind blows the encircling forest to a roar. Papers fly up and blind; a tire is blown from his hand. He scrambles the scrapiron pile to the shelter side, stands, coat flapping, blown riverspray wet on his face, hallooing and hallooing to the stone bears on the bridge, the bending trees.

Loony, loony, get down. You see that canvas needs tackin? Tack.

Miming Wes's face   Sounding Evans dry ghost cough   Gentling his bruised shoulder. Sometimes stopping whatever he is doing, his mouth opening: fixed to the look on her dying face

We'll be able to start burnin today or tomorrow if the wind stays down, says Wes. Don't this sun feel good? Just smell.

Brew of rose bay, forest, river, earth dryings, baked by the sun into a great fragrant steaminess. In it, every metal scrap, every piece of glass, glances, flashes, quivers, spangles, ripples light.

Wes stands in fountains of light: white sparkles as he moves the wheel for knife sharpening; blue jettings as he welds a radiator.

I didn't know you could sing, Stevie. You practicing for the Majors Amateur Hour?

It's for my head, Wes.

Outa your head, you mean.

The baking warmth, the vapor, the dazzle, the windlessness.

Toward noon the next day, they set the burn pile. Wes lets him douse on the gasoline, but the boy's look is so unnatural—spasms of laughing and spastic body dance as the flames spurt—Wes cuffs him away.

You a firebug nut or something? Get away, loony.

The wordless ecstasy will not contain. Quiver and dazzle are magnified in the strange smoking air. Baking mud sucks at his shoes as he runs from flash to flash. Stench of burning rubber and smoldering wet rags layer in with heady sweet spring vapors. How

vast each breath. Wreathes of yellow and black smoke rise. A stately
rain of ash begins. *And still the rippling, glancing, magnifying light.*
It drives him down by the river, but the stench and dazzle are there
too, and flashing rainbow crescents he does not know are salmon
leaping.

There, where the blue water greens the edging forest, the climbing
fir trees blue the sky, on a sandy spit, sun drenched, he lays himself
down.

Only when they turn at Panther Creek for the Requa cutoff do they
leave the smoke. They ride west into setting sun blare. The road is
gold, black leaves shake out sungold, and from the low deer brush—
outlined too in gilt—there reels a drunken wild-lilac smell.

Ten more days to huntin, Stevie. You don't know how much I want
them few days . . . I shouldn't have got so mad; you're doin almost
o.k. lately, sometimes as much help as trouble. Even your shootin

Four days in a half stupor, pumping for breath.

Why do you have to pull something like this for? Now I'll have
to work Decoration Day, be far enough ahead so he'll give me them
three days off . . .

Mrs. Ed, come here, isn't there anything you can do to help this
poor kid catch his breath?

———

He stands beside her negligently, as if he is not there at all, stooping
his newly tall, awkward body into itself while she introduces him to
the preacher, families, other young.

Better go in, Stephen, you shouldn't be standing here in this
strong wind. Betty'll show you where to sit, won't you, Betty?

    his Dad . . . never knew him . . . before he was
    born . . . AEF . . . a young woman, so sudden
    . . . Wes Davis   his uncle . . . all he has

His sleeves don't pull down to cover   ugly scabs   *That these dead shall not have*   peely walls   Mrs. Edler's arm light on his hurt shoulder   *He breaketh the bow and snappeth the spear asunder*   cobwebs under the backless benches   spiders?   his skin crawls   Scratching the itch places he can reach   scratching blood   Somebody giggling whispering

There is a fountain filled with blood
dead fly in the hymn book   sweet voice   a girl or lady in back
     and there may I, as vile as he   wash all my sins away
somebody giggling whispering   The sleeves don't pull down

———

At the first cemetery, he waits for her under the Requiescat in Pace gate. People come by, carrying wreaths and flowers and planting flags. If you were a dead soldier, you got a flag. The flags made crackle noises in the wind—like shooting practice—and kept getting blown down and having to be planted again.

A girl—that Betty maybe?—called his name, so he had to walk to a tangled part where nobody else was. His foot kicked over something—a glass canning jar—rust and dried things that might once have been flowers in it. Did it belong to the marble hand pointing to the sky, Leo Jordan, 1859–1911, He is Not Dead but Sleeping, or to the kneeling stone lamb, almost hidden by the tall blowing weeds?

He bent down and stood it by the lamb. Milena Willet was carved on it, 1 yr. old   Budded on earth
                    Blooming in Heaven
He had to pull away the weeds and scratch out sandy dirt to read the rest:

                    The mother strives in patient trust
                    Her bleeding heart to bow
                    For safe in God   the Good   the Just
                    Her babys sleeping now
That part was sunk in the ground.

How warm it felt down there in the weeds where nobody could see him and the wind didn't reach. The lamb was sun warm too. He put his arm around its stone neck and rested. Red ants threaded in and out; the smell was sweet like before they set the burn pile; even the crackling flags sounded far away.

The sleep stayed in him all the way to the second cemetery. Other people were in the car, they had stopped at back dirt roads to get them. You always get out and open the car door for ladies, Stephen, Mrs. Edler had said. But they weren't ladies, they were Indians.

The sun baked in through the car window and their trouble talk floated in haze   He says the law on his side   legal   *but it's ours*   the Sheriff   bones don't prove it he says the law

This cemetery he didn't get out of the car. It trembled all the time, pushed and rattled by the wind. Trees, bent all their lives that one way, clawed toward the windows. There were firing sounds here too, but maybe they were ocean booms. He thought he could see ocean, lashing beyond the trees.

———

What did you do to him? Wes asked Mrs. Edler. When I heard where you went, I expected sure he'd get back near dead, bad as in the beginning. But he's been frisky as a puppy all day. Chased me round the junk heaps. Rassled   went down to the river on his own   throwed skimmers   sharped a saw perfect   Paid attention   Curled up and fell asleep on the way home.

That's where he is—still sleeping. Lay down second we got home and I can't get him up. Blowing out the biggest bubble of snot you ever saw.   Just try and figger that loony kid.

stealthily   secretly reclaiming

Short Nonfiction From
and About the 1930s

A VISION OF FEAR AND HOPE

Sometimes the young—discouraged, overwhelmed—ask me incredulously: "You mean you still have hope?" And I hear myself saying, yes, I still have hope: beleaguered, starved, battered, based hope. Through horrors, blood, betrayals, apathy, callousness, retreats, defeats—in every decade of my now 82-year-old life that hope has been tested, affirmed. And more than hope: an exhaustless store of certainty, vision, belief—which came to me first in the time of my youthhood, the Depression '30s.

I live still with the ugliness of the decade: the degrading misery, the aloneness, the ravishing hunger, despair: the violence of the clubbings, gassings, jailings, the then shocking killing of swelling numbers of our countryfolk. I live, too, with the beauty of the decade: its affirmation of democracy and action; the new life given to assemble, petition, speak out; the use of the right to vote in unprecedented numbers (the first great attempt in the South to break the terror which kept black citizens from that right); the still unseen evidence of human greatness in words, spirit and deed; the burgeoning solidarity in the nation, bridging differences in color, background, creed, walk of life. Out of that visibility, that sense of identification, came our first body of literature, art, songs, photographs, film concerned with the lives and experiences of most of us.

For the first time, we began to have a sense of our country in all its hues, its wrongs and its rights, its unique diversity and likenesses, its pain, beauty, strengths, possibilities. We were no longer a country of individual helplessness and isolation. Millions in motion, acting together, might not always change their economic circumstances, but they could electrify the consciousness of the nation. And in 1932 we voted Franklin D. Roosevelt into office, who brought along with him not only Eleanor but also women (like Secretary of Labor Frances Perkins) and men of integrity with long histories of caring and public service.

Images were beginning to represent a decade: apples, the bread line, the migrant mother, the man with his sign, I WILL WORK FOR FOOD. The images helped rouse us to act, to say that hunger is morally wrong and that there must be another way. The familiar faces: pitted, seamed, lined, desperate, beaten, often shamed to be photographed with their poor possessions and their misery. But I also saw other expressions on such faces: stopping the evictions, putting the furniture back, on the picket lines, on the road, the pondering, questioning faces; the anguish not beaten.

Hard times indeed. No official figures were kept, but estimates were that about one fourth of the labor force (40 million human beings and their families) had no jobs or regular income. As Roosevelt said, "I see one third of a nation, ill-housed, ill-clad, ill-nourished." One of every four farms was foreclosed, and half a million farm families lived at starvation levels. At least a million transients—a third of them between 18 and 24 years old—were on the move, riding the "rattlers" to someplace that might be better. "Hoovervilles" were the human dumpheaps where nameless Frank Lloyd Wrights wrought their wondrous futuristic structures of flat battered tin cans, fruit boxes and gunny sacks, cardboard and mother earth, encrusting the banks of the rivers or mushrooming under the viaducts. Dog-kennel size, dog-kennel life. Sometimes shelter was any hole in the ground, covered with an old army coat or bit of canvas. One day in Sacramento, an old piecework quilt, already half rag, stunned me with its beauty, its feathering of colors, still lustrous in that freezing rain.

Many stories like that: The salt-pork relief—boiling it and boiling it to try to leach out the salt enough so we wouldn't gag on it. The bowl of coffee and milk, sometimes with three cinnamon buns, we lived on for a day. Corn-meal mush, beans if we could buy them, the pail of lard rancid. A neighbor in Stockton insisting that the family shacked up in the water tower behind us had eaten a stray dog.

I was jailed twice. First in Kansas City, winter, '32, for "making loud and unusual noises." I'd been working at Armour's and now distributed leaflets to meatpackers at Swift's, in a near blizzard, for the Young Communist League. Plenty of communists then, before it got so bitter and confusing abroad. Pushing for a 10-cent-an-hour raise was "communist inspired." I languished five or six weeks—no money for bail—and got pleurisy then incipient TB, which took me to Minnesota and out of the movement.

The second time was in San Francisco, right after a general strike. Perfect order we kept, marching up Market Street. Two longshoremen had been killed and more than 100,000 people came to pay tribute. No one spoke. The only sound was the beat of our feet. Then came "The Terror"—bloody crackdowns by vigilantes who, with police giving them the power to arrest, wrecked encampments and beat strikers and "sympathizers." No warrants, up the stairs, the thunder of their feet. Five of us jailed, I the only one of my sex. One was a student who didn't tell us he was a Reynolds tobacco heir. Another was a young seaman aspiring to be a writer. The police deliberately smashed his precious ancient typewriter.

I was a single mother then. In that pre-Pill time, even information on contraception was often illegal. Abortion was wholly illegal. Yet for the first time in our history, the birthrate was falling. How? Yes, there were secret, dangerous abortions—if one could find an abortionist, if one had the money. For those ignorant of their bodies there were these stratagems: turpentine, falling down stairs, lifting heavy furniture. The more informed tried a medication made from the ergot fungus. We still nursed each other's babies when needed.

Wages were cut in half. The workweek was six days. It was the era of the stretchout—sometimes called "The Beedo system"—in which the idea was to work one's employees to exhaustion in order to extract maximum profit out of the human body. At the beginning, there were few if any rights on the job to safety or against truly inhuman working conditions. An accident? Too bad. No responsibility by management. It took years of work to earn even one week's vacation. Unemployment was one's own fault. In March of '31 Henry Ford said, "There's plenty of work to do if people would do it." A few weeks later he laid off 75,000.

Most Americans alive then were not what is called well educated. At least 80 percent of us were out of school by the eighth grade. We were not the "best and the brightest." What we aspired to, struggled for and sometimes actually brought into being in the '30s was forming a new consciousness as to what the next great step for humanity must be—not only "the right to life, liberty and the pursuit of happiness" but the establishment of the means—the social, economic, cultural, educational means to give pulsing, enabling life to those rights. Seemingly disregarded, unknown by most, these are articulated in FDR's annual message to Congress in the month before we lost him, and more fully (in what Eleanor dedicated the remaining years of her life to) in the last portion of the 1948 Universal Declaration of Human Rights.

What transformed the '30s was that the president of the United States became part of our struggle. How simply and directly he spoke to us from the beginning: Relief, Recovery, Reform. "Our great primary task is to put people to work," he said. And he acted in a dazzling 100 days: banking reform, farm credits, the National Industrial Recovery Act (new jobs, reduced hours and raised wages). Later came insurance of bank deposits, Social Security and the Wagner Act, with its right to organize unions written into law, and much more.

FDR knew that the system was not working, that there was a correlation between the accepted, respected (fawned upon, cringed before) powerful in America and the brutality and corruption all around us. Roosevelt came from them, he understood them and he denounced them in terms so much more direct than his successors in office. Campaigning in 1936, he said: "We know that government by organized money is just as dangerous as government by organized mob." In a remarkable April 1938 address to Congress, he warned that "private enterprise is ceasing to be free enterprise," noting that 1 percent of the nation's corporations were taking 50 percent of the profits.

From the beginning, FDR moved and acted and spoke with us, and he did not call out the army or use his office to crush resistance. In Inaugural Addresses, State of the Union Messages, fireside chats, speeches, he always, always said hunger is wrong, joblessness is wrong. This was at a time when everything from a minimum wage to unemployment insurance was denounced as sovietizing the country, as the destruction of industry, as "un-American." Roosevelt's achievement was to redefine what being American meant. For all the New Deal legislation and regulation, the decade ended with the same crowd in power and in profit, but they now had to contend with a federal government that consistently intervened on the side of the people.

FDR genuinely believed in capitalism, and he saved it. Yet he grew and changed, and especially with the help of Eleanor he connected to larger themes of human rights. Some of us, bruised by the Fascist victory in the Spanish Civil War in 1936, were ahead of him in anticipating the conflict to come. But he was ahead of most of the country in preparing for war.

Today, the vision of full humanhood is battered, scorned, deemed "unrealistic." But I still remember what people can achieve when we act together. The 1930s were full of torture and brutality, but in this country, at least, history was more than a boot in the face. It was a time of human flowering, when the country was transformed by the hopes, dreams, actions of numerous, nameless human beings, hungry for more than food.

1994

THE STRIKE

Do not ask me to write of the strike and the terror. I am on a battle-field, and the increasing stench and smoke sting the eyes so it is impossible to turn them back into the past. You leave me only this night to drop the bloody garment of Todays, to cleave through the gigantic events that have crashed one upon the other, to the first beginning. If I could go away for a while, if there were time and quiet, perhaps I could do it. All that has happened might resolve into order and sequence, fall into neat patterns of words. I could stumble back into the past and slowly, painfully rear the structure in all its towering magnificence, so that the beauty and heroism, the terror and significance of those days, would enter your heart and sear it forever with the vision.

But I hunch over the typewriter and behind the smoke, the days whirl, confused as dreams. Incidents leap out like a thunder and are gone. There flares the remembrance of that night in early May, in Stockton, when I walked down the road with the paper in my hands and the streaming headlines, LONGSHOREMEN OUT. RIOT EX-

PECTED; LONGSHORE STRIKE DECLARED. And standing there in the yellow stubble I remember Jerry telling me quietly, ". . . for 12 years now. But we're through sweating blood, loading cargo five times the weight we should carry, we're through standing morning after morning like slaves in a slave market begging for a bidder. We'll be out, you'll see; it may be a few weeks, a few months, but WE'LL BE OUT, and then hell can't stop us."

H-E-L-L C-A-N-T S-T-O-P U-S. Days, pregnant days, spelling out the words. The port dead but for the rat stirring of a few scabs at night, the port paralyzed, gummed on one side by the thickening scum of prostate ships, islanded on the other by the river of pickets streaming ceaselessly up and down, a river that sometimes raged into a flood, surging over the wavering shoreline of police, battering into the piers and sucking under the scabs in its angry tides. HELL CAN'T STOP US. That was the meaning of the lines of women and children marching up Market with their banners—"This is our fight, and we're with the men to the finish." That was the meaning of the seamen and the oilers and the wipers and the mastermates and the pilots and the scalers torrenting into the river, widening into the sea.

The kids coming in from the waterfront. The flame in their eyes, the feeling of invincibility singing in their blood. The stories they had to tell of scabs educated, of bloody skirmishes. My heart was ballooning with happiness anyhow, to be back, working in the movement again, but the things happening down at the waterfront, the heroic everydays, stored such richness in me I can never lose it. The feeling of sympathy widening over the city, of quickening—class lines sharpening. I armored myself with that on National Youth Day hearing the smash and thud of clubs around me, seeing boys fall to their knees in streams of blood, pioneer kids trampled under by horses. . . .

There was a night that was the climax of those first days—when the workers of San Francisco packed into the Auditorium to fling a warning to the shipowners. There are things one holds like glow in the breast, like a fire; they make the unseen warmth that keeps one through the cold of defeat, the hunger of despair. That night was one—symbol and portent of what will be. We League kids came to the meeting in a group, and walking up the stairs we felt ourselves a flame, a force. At the door bulls were standing, with menacing faces, but behind them fear was blanching—the people massing in, they had never dreamed it possible—people coming in and filling the aisles, packing the back. Spurts of song flaming up from downstairs, answered by us, echoed across the gallery, solidarity weaving us all into one being. 20,000 jammed in and the dim blue ring of cops back in the hall was wavering, was stretching itself thin and unseeable. It was OUR auditorium, we had taken it over. And for blocks around they hear OUR voice. The thunder of our applause, the mighty roar of it for Bridges, for Caves, for Schumacher. "That's no lie." "Tell them Harry" "To the Finish" "We're with you" "Attaboy" "We're solid." The speeches, "They can never load their ships with tear gas and guns," "For years we were nothing but nameless beasts of burden to them, but now. . . ." "Even if it means . . . GENERAL STRIKE," the voices rising, lifted on a sea of affection, vibrating in 20,000 hearts.

There was the moment—the first bruise in the hearts of our mas-ters—when Mayor Rossi entered, padding himself from the fists of boos smashing around him with 60 heavyfoots, and bulls, and honoraries. The boos had filled into breasts feeling and seeing the tattoo of his clubs on the embarcadero, and Rossi hearing tried to lose himself into his topcoat, failing, tried to puff himself invincible with the majesty of his office. "Remember, I am your chief executive, the respect . . . the honor . . . due that office . . . don't listen to me then but listen to your mayor . . . listen," and the boos rolled over him again and again so that the reptile voice smothered, stopped. He never forgot the moment he called for law and order, charging the meeting with not caring to settle by peaceful means, wanting only violence, and voices ripped from every corner. "Who started the violence?" "Who calls the bulls to the waterfront?" "Who ordered the clubbing?"—and in a torrent of anger shouted, "Shut up, we have to put up with your clubs but not with your words, get out of here, GET OUT OF HERE." That memory clamped into his heart, into the hearts of those who command him, that bruise became the cancer of fear that flowered into the monstrous Bloody Thursday, that opened into the pus of Terror—but the cancer grows, grows; there is no cure. . . .

It was after that night he formed his "Citizens Committee," after that night the still smiling lips of the Industrial Association bared into a growl of open hatred, exposing the naked teeth of guns and tear gas. The tempo of those days maddened to a crescendo. The city became a camp, a battlefield, the screams of ambulances sent the day reeling, class lines fell sharply—everywhere, on streetcars, on corners, in stores, people talked, cursing, stirred with something strange in their breasts, incomprehensible, shaken with fury at the police, the papers, the shipowners . . . going down to the waterfront, not curious spectators, but to stand there, watching, silent, trying to read the lesson the moving bodies underneath were writing, trying to grope to the meaning of it all, police "protecting lives" smashing clubs and gas bombs into masses of men like themselves, papers screaming lies. Those were the days when with every attack on the picket lines the phone rang at the I.L.A.—"NOW—will you arbitrate?"—when the mutter GENERAL STRIKE swelled to a thunder, when everywhere the cry arose—"WE'VE GOT TO END IT NOW." Coming down to headquarters from the waterfront, the faces of comrades had the strained look of men in battle, that strangely intense look of living, of feeling too much in too brief a space of time. . . .

Yes, those were the days crescendoing—and the typewriter breaks, stops for an instant—to Bloody Thursday. Weeks afterward my fists clench at the remembrance and the hate congests so I feel I will burst. Bloody Thursday—our day we write on the pages of history with letters of blood and hate. Our day we fling like a banner to march with the other bloody days when guns spat death at us that a few dollars might be saved to fat bellies, when lead battered into us, and only our naked hands, the fists of our bodies moving together could resist. Drown their strength in blood, they commanded, but instead they armored us in inflexible steel—hate that will never forget. . . .

"It was a close to war . . . as actual war could be," the papers blared triumphantly, but Bridges told them, "not war . . . MASSA-CRE, armed forces massacreing unarmed." Words I read through tears of anger so that they writhed and came alive like snakes, you rear in me again, "and once again the policemen, finding their gas bombs and gas shells ineffective poured lead from their revolvers into the jammed streets. Men (MEN) fell right and left." ". . . And everywhere was the sight of men, beaten to their knees to lie in a pool of blood." "Swiftly, from intersection to intersection the battle moved, stubbornly the rioters refused to fall back so that the police were forced . . ." "and the police shot forty rounds of tear gas bombs into the mob before it would move. . . ."

Law . . . and order . . . will . . . prevail. Do you hear? It's war, WAR—and up and down the street "A man clutched at his leg and fell to the sidewalk" "The loud shot like that of the tear gas bombs zoomed again, but no blue smoke this time, and when the men cleared, two bodies lay on the sidewalk, their blood trickling about them."—overhead an airplane lowered, dipped, and nausea gas swooned down in a cloud of torture, and where they ran from street to street, resisting stubbornly, massing again, falling back only to carry the wounded, the thought tore frenziedly through the mind, war, war, it's WAR—and the lists in the papers, the dead, the wounded by bullets, the wounded by other means—W-A-R.

LAW—you hear, Howard Sperry, exserviceman, striking stevedore, shot in the back and abdomen, said to be in dying condition, DEAD, LAW AND ORDER—you hear and remember this Ben Martella, shot in arm, face and chest, Joseph Beovich, stevedore, laceration of skull from clubbing and broken shoulder, Edwin Hodges, Jerry Hart, Leslie Steinhart, Steve Hamrock, Albert Simmons, marine engineer, striking seamen, scaler, innocent bystander, shot in leg, shot in shoulder, chest lacerated by tear gas shell, gassed in eyes, compound skull fracture by clubbing, you hear—LAW AND ORDER MUST PREVAIL—it's all right Nick, clutching your leg and seeing through the fog of pain it is a police car has picked you up, snarling, let me out, I don't want any bastard bulls around, and flinging yourself out into the street, still lying there in the hospital today—

LAW AND ORDER—people, watching with horror, trying to comprehend the lesson the moving bodies were writing. The man stopping me on the corner, seeing my angry tears as I read the paper, "Listen," he said, and he talked because he had to talk, because in an hour all the beliefs in his life had been riddled and torn away— "Listen, I was down there, on the waterfront, do you know what they're doing—they were shooting SHOOTING—" and that word came out anguished and separate, "shooting right into men, human beings, they were shooting into them as if they were animals, as if they were targets, just lifting their guns and shooting. I saw this, can you believe it, CAN YOU BELIEVE IT? . . . as if they were targets as if . . . CAN YOU BELIEVE IT?" and he went to the next man and started it all over again. . . .

I was not down . . . by the battlefield. My eyes are anguished from the pictures I pieced together from words of comrades, of strikers, from the pictures filling the newspapers. I sat up in headquarters, racked by the howls of ambulances hurling by, feeling it incredible the fingers like separate little animals hopping nimbly from key to key, the ordered steady click of the typewriter, feeling any moment the walls would crash and all the madness surge in. Ambulances, ripping out of nowhere, fading; police sirens, outside the sky a ghastly gray, corpse gray, an enormous dead eyelid shutting down on the world. And someone comes in, words lurch out of his mouth, the skeleton is told, and goes again. . . . And I sit there, making a metallic little pattern of sound in the air, because that is all I can do, because that is what I am supposed to do.

They called the guard out . . . "admitting their inability to control the situation," and Barrows boasted, "my men will not use clubs or gas, they will talk with bayonets" . . . Middlestaedt . . . "Shoot to kill. Any man firing into the air will be courtmartialed." With two baby tanks, and machine guns, and howitzers, they went down to the waterfront to take it over, to "protect the interests of the people."

I walked down Market that night. The savage wind lashed at my hair. All life seemed blown out of the street; the few people hurrying by looked hunted, tense, expectant of anything. Cars moved past as if fleeing. And a light, indescribably green and ominous was cast over everything, in great shifting shadows. And down the street the trucks rumbled. Drab colored, with boys sitting on them like corpses sitting and not moving, holding guns stiffly, staring with wide frightened eyes, carried down to the Ferry building, down to the Embarcadero to sell out their brothers and fathers for $2.00 a day. Somebody said behind me, and I do not even know if the voice was my own, or unspoken, or imagined, "Go on down there, you sonovabitches, it doesn't matter. It doesn't stop us. We won't forget what happened today. . . . Go on, nothing can stop us . . . now."

Somehow I am down on Stuart and Mission, somehow I am staring at flowers scattered in a border over a space of sidewalk, at stains that look like rust, at an unsteady chalking—"Police Murder. Two Shot in the Back," and looking up I see faces, seen before, but utterly changed, transformed by some inner emotion to faces of steel. "Nick Bordoise . . . and Sperry, on the way to punch his strike card, shot in the back by those bastard bulls. . . ."

Our Brothers

Howard S. Sperry, a longshoreman, a war vet, a real MAN. On strike since May 9th, 1934 for the right to earn a decent living under decent conditions. . . . Nickolas Bordoise, a member of Cooks & Waiters Union for ten years. Also a member of the International Labor Defense. Not a striker, but a worker looking to the welfare of his fellow workers on strike. . . .

Some of what the leaflet said. But what can be said of Howard Sperry, exserviceman, struggling through the horrors of war for his country, remembering the dead men and the nearly dead men lashing about blindly on the battlefield, who came home to die in a new war, a war he had not known existed. What can be said of Nick Bordoise. Communist Party member, who without thanks or request came daily to the embarcadero to sell his fellow workers hot soup to warm their bellies. There was a voice that gave the story of his life, there in the yellowness of the parched grass, with the gravestones icy and strange in the sun; quietly, as if it had risen up from the submerged hearts of the world, as if it had been forever and would be forever, the voice surged over our bowed heads. And the story was the story of any worker's life, of the thousand small deprivations and frustrations suffered, of the courage forged out of the cold and darkness of poverty, of the determination welded out of the helpless anger scalding the heart, the plodding hours of labor and weariness, of the life, given simply, as it had lived, that the things which he had suffered should not be, must not be. . . .

There were only a few hundred of us who heard that voice, but the thousands who watched the trucks in the funeral procession piled high with 50¢ and $1.00 wreaths guessed, and understood. I saw the people, I saw the look on their faces. And it is the look that will be there the days of the revolution. I saw the fists clenched till knuckles were white, and people standing, staring, saying nothing, letting it clamp into their hearts, hurt them so the scar would be there forever—a swelling that would never let them lull.

"Life," the capitalist papers marveled again, "Life stopped and stared." Yes, you stared, our cheap executive, Rossi—hiding behind the curtains, the cancer of fear in your breast gnawing, gnawing; you stared, members of the Industrial Association, incredulous, where did the people come from, where was San Francisco hiding them, in what factories, what docks, what are they doing there, marching, or standing and watching, not saying anything, just watching. . . . What did it mean, and you dicks, fleeing, hiding behind store windows. . . .

There was a pregnant woman standing on a corner, outlined against the sky, and she might have been a marble, rigid, eternal, expressing some vast and nameless sorrow. But her face was a flame, and I heard her say after a while dispassionately, as if it had been said so many times no accent was needed, "We'll not forget that. We'll pay it back . . . someday." And on every square of sidewalk a man was saying, "We'll have it. We'll have a General Strike. And there won't be processions to bury their dead." "Murder—to save themselves paying a few pennies more wages, remember that Johnny . . . We'll get even. It won't be long. General Strike."

Listen, it is late, I am feverish and tired. Forgive me that the words are feverish and blurred. You see, If I had time, If I could go away. But I write this on a battlefield.

The rest, the General Strike, the terror, arrests and jail, the songs in the night, must be written some other time, must be written later. . . . But there is so much happening now. . . .

THOUSAND-DOLLAR VAGRANT

It was Lincoln Steffens who commanded me to write this story. "People don't know," he informed me, "how they arrest you, what they say, what happens in court. Tell them. Write it just as you told me about it." So here it is.

I would have left at nine-thirty, but Billy came in with a thrilling story of how out in Fillmore the telephone poles had been plastered with leaflets, with stickers, "The Communist Party Lives and Fights." And for the first time in days, the strain, the sense of breaking over the heart, had slackened, disappeared. Sitting there, with the lulling simmer of the teakettle, the blinds drawn, safe, secure, I forgot the papers with their ugly headlines, the plainclothes dicks standing on every corner looking and waiting, the police cars rattling over the city, the screams of ambulances. I went over and began to wash the dishes. And someone knocked on the door.

Bill came back. "Bulls," he said, "get Johnny out first." For a second we stood and stared—then ducked Johnny out the back door. Then we dashed ourselves. But ugly voices were shouting, "Hold it, hold it, or we'll plug you," and the rods were pointed at us.

Johnny had got away. Billy, Jack, Dave and I were left. They rounded us back into the kitchen. There were five of them. Only the two harness bulls looked a little human. The other faces were distorted and bestial. I wouldn't have been surprised if they had ripped out knives or irons and started torturing us, if their revolvers had been pulled out and gone off. Words were lurching out of the head bull's mouth. His small pig eyes floated in red puddles. I gathered he was telling us to move over against the wall. Dave wasn't fast enough for him. He whipped out a blackjack and beat Dave over the head and chest.

They began searching the place. Flinging up curtains, peering in the garbage can, looking in the stove, ransacking the drawers. Questions ripped at us. "Who are you, what's your name, were you born in Russia, who else was here, did anybody get away, who you expectin'?"

They asked Jack: "You a Communist?"

"Yes," he answered, "that's legal, isn't it?"

"Yeah? You're gonna find out how legal that is, you red bastard. This country's not good enough for you, huh? You don't like our Constitution, huh?"

A harness bull comes in from the other room with a box of Sam's books—at the same moment one of the plainclothes dicks discovers the bulletin the kids had been working on, stuck in a pan on the wall.

The head bull reads the names of the books. He takes out "Murder at Camp Hohenzollern" and—excitedly—Adamic's "Dynamite." "What you been planning to dynamite?" he thunders at Jack. "You know?"—he asks each of us—"You? You?"

They tell me to go into the other room. I am glad to sit down. I know they want me out of the kitchen. I hear the questions. "Where were you born? In Russia?" Silence, a thud of something soft on a body. "What you doing here?" Silence. A thud. "Who's the girl?" Silence. A thud. "Where do you live? You? How many times you been arrested? Who's the head guy around here? What nationality are you? Come on—lie, we know you're all Jews or greasers or niggers. Who do you live with?"

The gorilla leaves the others to do the questioning and the slugging and comes into the other room. "What's your name?" "Teresa Landale." "Your address?" I can't give mine. "37 Grove," I answer. "What?" he bellows, "that's the Western—Western Striker address." (Western Worker.) "What do you do for a living?" "I'm a writer." "A writer?" He calls over to a weasel-faced bull—"Hey, we got the editor of The Western Striker." I protest. In vain. From now on I am editor of The Western Striker. "You married?" I don't answer. "You're Jack Olson's girl aren't you? Aren't you?" I don't answer. "What you doing here?" "I came to do a little typing." "Ever been arrested before? ... Who's the other guys? Who got away? You're a Communist, ain't you? You know what would've happened if we wouldn't 've come. You'd probably been raped. Don't you know these guys aren't any better than niggers?"

I sat for three hours in the drafty central police station waiting for the black maria to take us over to the jail. There they registered us, searched the boys, and gave them another work-over (the kind of beating that hurts but doesn't show). While they were searching and registering the boys, I sat in one of the offices—trying to listen to a cop question me about the money that came from Russia. I heard afterward that when the desk sergeant commented on the fact that Billy only had a nickel and two pennies in his pocket, Billy told him gravely the strike had tied up our last three shipments of Moscow gold. This cop evidently believed it.

When they registered me, I gave my address as 71 Diamond. A nonexistent number. Immediately, two plainclothesmen were sent out to investigate it and raid the place. I was again questioned about my name, means of support, relatives, etc. "If you tell me, it'll prove you're not a vagrant."

But it doesn't matter who you are—you're helpless. If you give any names of members of your family they see that they lose their jobs; if you give your address they raid the place and wreck the furniture in the process of "searching." And even if you do show your "visible means of support"—you're still a vagrant. One of the boys' last paycheck was in his pocket, and Marion Chandler had been arrested while she was sick in bed in her own home—as a vagrant. They got Mink and Sam too, who had rented the place. It was the landlady who had spotted it—the clicking of the typewriter at night, and the blinds pulled down, had made her suspicious.

The parting words to us as we got into the black maria were these: "This is your last ride for a long time—till you get to the county jail. You'll go up before Steiger and ask for a jury trial and get $1,000 bail clamped on you, and you'll get your trial—and you'll lie around and rot till you do, and you'll be convicted—and then we'll take the whole bunch of you, pour oil over you, and burn you up like they do the niggers down south."

It's a nice jail. The prostitutes say it's the nicest city jail in the United States. The matrons are nice too. When one searched my pockets and shoes, she apologized, saying it was the routine procedure. The fingerprint guy was human too. He was the first one who hadn't refused to believe anything I said, who didn't have me down as a (1) Communist, (2) liar, (3) foreigner, because I had happened to be with several Communists when a place was raided. He asked me to tell him—honestly—if I believed in this Communism, didn't I know it was all anarchy, rape, and bloodshed? Didn't I know it was controlled in Russia? Didn't I realize how it would ruin my life to be mixed up with such a bunch—here I was fingerprinted, down for life as a criminal, etc. . . .

The women's side of the jail was crowded that night, so girls were sleeping two in a bunk, four in a cell. But over on the men's side they were so crowded it was impossible to lie down. The first night I slept on a mattress on the floor. In the morning, when everyone filed in, I discovered there were three more $1,000 vagrants. Two of them were Communists; the third, Marion Chandler, was the wife of a Communist active in the unemployed movement. Elaine, the secretary of the I.L.D., told me not to answer questions, and to refuse to take quarantine. For I discovered that Steiger had placed Marion under quarantine (tests for syphilis and gonorrhea given to prostitutes) and had thundered she'd stay in jail until she submitted. She didn't, and nothing was said when she got out on bail. Though the quarantine charge was slated for me too, not a word was said about it.

At ten in the morning, I marched down to police court with the prostitutes, the drunks and a woman who had tried to kill her lover. They brought down the boys, handcuffed, behind us. We were up before Judge Steiger—the most bitter anti-labor judge in California. He has two idols—the first is Brisbane, and he drains every opportunity to say some resounding vacuity he considers scathing, or some maudlin platitude he considers profound; the second is Hitler. When Billy, in order to protect his parents, refused to say he had been in touch with them the past three years, Steiger, almost weeping, delivered an encomium on the filial virtues, the sympathy he felt for the poor parents whose son Communism had turned into a viper; to Dave, who said he had a teacher's certificate from the University of California, he bewailed the usages Communists put education to—taking advantage of our free schools, and then turning against the very government that makes their education possible.

When I refused to answer any questions other than that I was born in Nebraska, he suggested they investigate my sanity, only a mental case could talk like that. And he meant it. On all of us he put the usual $1,000 bail. Absolutely no proof was offered that I was a Communist, no one had ever seen me before, but the mere fact that I was at the moment in company with some was enough to convince him.

Jack had evidently made a brief outline of what should go into a bulletin the Young Communist League was going to put out. On it he had a list something like—National Guard, Bernal Heights Story, the San Jose Terror, etc. Steiger had it on top of the "evidence"—the confiscated papers; his face glowed with delight—"incriminating stuff. Evidently code. Very dangerous. This is good work—these papers are valuable to us." When we went up before Judge Jacks to have our bail reduced, the judge declared, "Unfortunately Communism is no crime—as yet, though every other type of insanity allows us to place the culprit behind the bars. Communism is the effusion of halfwits. But do you have documents to prove they advocate overthrowing the government by force? That is a crime, you know." The officer announced he did. The judge read a marked paragraph out of a leaflet aloud once, twice. "Is that—can that be what you mean?" he asked. "Yah," the bull answered proudly, "there where it says to take over everything: 'Let the rank and file take control in their own hands, else there will be a sellout.'"

When I came up before the judge for bail reduction and he said, "so it was after you received the benefits of our free education that you decided our ideas weren't good enough, and you became a Communist," I answered—

"No, not then. It's since my free education gleaned during the last few days that I've got leanings in that direction."

I WANT YOU WOMEN UP NORTH TO KNOW

Based on a letter by Felipe Ibarro in *New Masses*, January 9th, 1934.

I want you women up north to know
how those dainty children's dresses you buy
    at macy's, wannamakers, gimbels, marshall fields,
are dyed in blood, are stitched in wasting flesh,
down in San Antonio, "where sunshine spends the winter."

I want you women up north to see
the obsequious smile, the salesladies trill
    "exquisite work, madame, exquisite pleats"
vanish into a bloated face, ordering more dresses,
    gouging the wages down,
dissolve into maria, ambrosia, catalina,
    stitching these dresses from dawn to night,
    In blood, in wasting flesh.

Catalina Rodriguez, 24,
    body shrivelled to a child's at twelve,
catalina rodriguez, last stages of consumption,
    works for three dollars a week from dawn to midnight.
A fog of pain thickens over her skull, the parching heat
    breaks over her body,
and the bright red blood embroiders the floor of her room.
    White rain stitching the night, the bourgeois poet would say.
    white gulls of hands, darting, veering,
    white lightning, threading the clouds,
this is the exquisite dance of her hands over the cloth,
and her cough, gay, quick, staccato,
    like skeleton's bones clattering,
is appropriate accompaniment for the esthetic dance
    of her fingers,
and the tremolo, tremolo when the hands tremble with pain.
Three dollars a week,
two fifty-five,
seventy cents a week,
no wonder two thousand eight hundred ladies of joy
are spending the winter with the sun after he goes down—
for five cents (who said this was a rich man's world?) you can
    get all the lovin you want
"clap and syph ain't much worse than sore fingers, blind eyes, and
    t.b."

Maria Vasquez, spinster,
    for fifteen cents a dozen stitches garments for children she
    has never had,
Catalina Torres, mother of four,
    to keep the starved body starving, embroiders from dawn
    to night.
Mother of four, what does she think of,
    as the needle pocked fingers shift over the silk—

of the stubble-coarse rags that stretch on her own brood,
and jut with the bony ridge that marks hunger's landscape
of fat little prairie-roll bodies that will bulge in the
silk she needles?
(Be not envious, Catalina Torres, look!
on your own children's clothing, embroidery,
more intricate than any a thousand hands could fashion,
there where the cloth is raveled, or darned,
designs, multitudinous, complex and handmade by Poverty
herself.)
Ambrosa Espinoza trusts in god,
"Todos es de dios, everything is from god,"
through the dwindling night, the waxing day, she bolsters
herself up with it—
but the pennies to keep god incarnate, from ambrosa,
and the pennies to keep the priest in wine, from ambrosa,
ambrosa clothes god and priest with hand-made children's
dresses.

Her brother lies on an iron cot, all day and watches,
on a mattress of rags he lies.
For twenty-five years he worked for the railroad, then they laid
him off.
(racked days, searching for work; rebuffs; suspicious eyes of
policemen.
goodbye ambrosa, mebbe in dallas I find work; desperate
swing for a freight,
surprised hands, clutching air, and the wheel goes over a
leg,
the railroad cuts it off, as it cut off twenty-five years of his
life.)
She says that he prays and dreams of another world, as he lies
there, a heaven (which he does not know was brought to
earth in 1917 in Russia, by workers like him).

Women up north, I want you to know
when you finger the exquisite hand-made dresses
what it means, this working from dawn to midnight,
on what strange feet the feverish dawn must come
    to maria, catalina, ambrosa,
how the malignant fingers twitching over the pallid faces jerk
them to work,
and the sun and the fever mount with the day—
    long plodding hours, the eyes burn like coals, heat jellies
    the flying fingers,
down comes the night like blindness.
    long hours more with the dim eye of the lamp, the breaking
    back,
    weariness crawls in the flesh like worms, gigantic like earth's
    in winter.
And for Catalina Rodriguez comes the night sweat and the blood
    embroidering the darkness.
    for Catalina Torres the pinched faces of four huddled
    children,
    the naked bodies of four bony children,
    the chant of their chorale of hunger.
And for twenty eight hundred ladies of joy the grotesque act gone
    over—the wink—the grimace—the "feeling like it baby?"
And for Maria Vasquez, spinster, emptiness, emptiness,
    flaming with dresses for children she can never fondle.
And for Ambrosa Espinoza—the skeleton body of her brother on
his mattress of rags, boring twin holes in the dark with his eyes
to the image of christ, remembering a leg, and twenty five years
cut off from his life by the railroad.

Women up north, I want you to know,
I tell you this can't last forever.

I swear it won't.

BIOGRAPHICAL SKETCH

Laurie Olsen and Julie Olsen Edwards

Tillie Lerner was born on a tenant farm in Nebraska, the second of six children of Russian Jewish immigrants who left their homeland after involvement in the failed 1905 revolution. She grew up in Omaha, where her father worked as a painter and paperhanger and served as state secretary in the Nebraska Socialist Party. Tillie was strongly influenced by her parents' revolutionary heritage and by their humanist and socialist beliefs. From a young age Tillie was a voracious reader, and though she dropped out of high school after the eleventh grade, ending her "formal" education, she remained a lifelong scholar—haunting public libraries and reading widely. In her words, "Public libraries were my sustenance and my college."

In 1929 she embarked on what would be thirty years of low-paying jobs (hotel maid, packinghouse worker, linen checker, waitress, laundry worker, factory worker, secretary). An activist and a member of the Young Communist League, Tillie became involved in the labor, social, and political causes of Depression-era Nebraska, Kansas, Missouri, and Minnesota. She was jailed for organizing packinghouse workers. It was while recovering from pleurisy and tuberculosis contracted as a result of factory conditions and weeks in jail that she began to write her first novel, *Yonnondio: From the Thirties*, which would not be published until forty years later.

In 1932 her first daughter, Karla, was born, and the next year they moved to San Francisco. In the San Francisco General Strike of 1934, Tillie was jailed on "Bloody Thursday," along with the man who would become her lifelong partner—Jack Olsen, a waterfront warehouseman, union organizer, and educator who shared her commitment to human rights and the struggle for justice, as well as her wide-ranging love of music and the arts. Two poems and a series of reports written in the course of that historic strike and published in the *New Republic* and the *Partisan Review* brought Tillie's writing to national attention; she was one of a few beginning writers invited to attend the American Writers Congress of 1935 in New York City.

Settling in San Francisco's Mission district, Jack and Tillie raised their four daughters, Karla, Julie, Kathie, and Laurie, and their home became a refuge and gathering place for people from all walks of life who shared their values and commitment to build a more just world. Although the conditions of working-class life and raising a family did not permit Olsen to pursue her writing for many years, the desire to write never left her. She continued to keep notebooks and to write on tiny slips of paper, in her words, "capturing voices, words, thoughts."

Throughout her life, Tillie was a familiar and passionate presence in community meetings, on picket lines, and at demonstrations. She organized for parks and playgrounds, was a founder of the city's first Parent Cooperative Nursery School, became a leader in the PTA, and during World War II served as director of the California CIO War Relief and president of the Women's Auxiliary of the CIO. She spoke out for labor, against apartheid and racism, as part of antiwar movements, on behalf of women's rights, to create a strong public education and public library system, and for the protection of the earth.

During the McCarthy era, Olsen was accused by a local zealot of being an "agent of Stalin working to infiltrate the city's schools through the PTA." Though Tillie was never charged, Jack was subpoenaed to appear before the House Committee on Un-American Activities—which lost him his job and ushered in years of renewed financial difficulty for the family.

In 1954, at the age of forty-two, Tillie returned to writing by taking a class at San Francisco State College. Encouraged by her teachers there, she applied for and received a Wallace Stegner Fellowship in Creative Writing at Stanford University; shortly afterward, at the age of forty-three, she published the short story "I Stand Here Ironing." Over the next eight years, she produced the four stories that were collected in her distinguished volume *Tell Me a Riddle*. "I Stand Here Ironing" was selected for *Best American Short Stories* of 1957. The title story of *Tell Me a Riddle* received the 1961 O. Henry Award as well as being included in *Best American Short Stories* for that year.

In 1959 she received a grant from the Ford Foundation to enable her to continue writing. Over the next few years, Olsen was fortunate to gain residencies at the MacDowell Colony, Yaddo, the Huntington Hartford Foundation, the Banff Center for the Arts, and other havens for writers throughout the country. She began work on "Requa I," which was selected for inclusion in *Best American Short Stories* of 1971.

During this era, mindful of her "hatred for all that . . . slows, impairs, silences writers," Olsen continued her activism and efforts to encourage other women and working-class writers to find their own voice, creativity, and expression. Correspondence with her fellow writers became extensive and continued throughout her life.

In 1970 Olsen was instrumental in founding the Feminist Press (now the Feminist Press at the City University of New York). She championed the republication of the nineteenth-century *Life in the Iron Mills* by Rebecca Harding Davis, writing an extended biographical afterword and inaugurating the Feminist Press's reprints of "lost" American classics by women writers.

Between 1969 and 1974, Olsen taught at Stanford University, the Massachusetts Institute of Technology, the University of Massachusetts, and served as the first woman "visiting writer" at Amherst College. Olsen's reading lists and syllabi for her classes became essential parts of the women's studies and American literary canon.

Olsen's nonfiction book *Silences* was published in 1978, examining the critical links between economic class, race, and gender that have prevented so many writers from writing. *Mother to Daughter—Daughter to Mother*, a daybook of quotations illuminating those relationships, was published to acclaim in 1993.

Her work has been anthologized in hundreds of volumes and made into three films and two stage plays. Her stories continue to be used in high schools, colleges, and universities around the world. She was awarded many distinguished fellowships and awards for her writing, as well as for her contributions to literature and for her activism. The plaque she kept on her wall, however, was an honorary high school diploma from Omaha Central High, given at the time of her honoring at the University of Nebraska.

With their children grown, Jack and Tillie moved to and lived for twenty years in the Western Addition of San Francisco in the St. Francis Square Cooperative Housing Project, built by the International Longshore and Warehousemen's Union in "the belief that people of all races and walks of life can live together in harmony." Throughout the 1980s and 1990s, Tillie was a familiar figure in the Western Addition and Tenderloin, handing out leaflets or posters, taking brisk walks, and stopping to talk with the homeless.

In recognition of Tillie's enormous contribution to the life of the city, then mayor Dianne Feinstein and the San Francisco Board of Supervisors declared a citywide Tillie Olsen Day in 1981. In 1998 she was similarly honored by the city of Santa Cruz, where she wrote and lived for several years.

In 1989 Tillie's lifelong partner, Jack Olsen, passed away. Tillie then moved to Berkeley, California, to be near her family. She lived there until her death on January 1, 2007, two weeks shy of her ninety-fifth birthday. Tillie Olsen's papers are archived at Stanford University in their Special Collections at the Green Library.

AWARDS AND HONORS

Olsen received honorary PhDs from: University of Nebraska (1979); Knox College (1982); Hobart & William Smith College (1984); Clark University (1985); Albright College (1986); Wooster College (1991); Mills College (1995); and Amherst College (1998). Major awards include: the Los Angeles Times Robert Kirsch Lifetime Achievement Award (2000); a Distinguished Achievement Award from the Western Literary Association (1996); the REA Award for Distinguished Contribution to the Short Story (1994); the Nebraska Library Association Mari Sandoz Award (1991); National Endowment for the Humanities grants (1984 and 1966); the Unitarian Women's Federation Award (1980); the American Academy and Institute of Arts and Letters Award for Distinguished Contribution to American Literature (1975); and a Guggenheim fellowship (1975). Other fellowships and awards include those from the Radcliffe Institute for Independent Study and the British Post Office, as well as the Stanford University Wallace Stegner Creative Writing Fellowship and the Bay Area Book Reviewers Fred Cody Lifetime Achievement Award.

SOURCE ACKNOWLEDGMENTS

All material reproduced by agreement with the Tillie Olsen Trust.

"I Stand Here Ironing" was previously published in *Pacific Spectator* 10 (Winter 1956): 55–63. Reprinted in *Best American Short Stories*, ed. Martha Foley (Boston: Houghton Mifflin, 1957).

"Hey Sailor, What Ship?" was originally published in *New Campus Writing*, ed. Nolan Miller (New York: Bantam, 1957).

"O Yes" was first published as "Baptism" in *Prairie Schooner* 31 (Spring 1957): 70–80.

"Tell Me a Riddle" was originally published in *New World Writing* 16 (1960): 11–57. Reprinted in *Best American Short Stories*, ed. Martha Foley and David Burnett (Boston: Houghton Mifflin, 1961).

"Requa I" was previously published in the *Iowa Review* 1 (Summer 1970): 54–74. Reprinted in *Best American Short Stories*, ed. Martha Foley and David Burnett (Boston: Houghton Mifflin, 1971), and in *Granta: New American Writing* (September 1979): 111–32.

"A Vision of Fear and Hope" was originally published in *Newsweek*, January 3, 1994, 26–27.

"The Strike" was originally published in *Partisan Review* 1 (September–October 1934): 3–9. Reprinted in *Years of Protest: A Collection of American Writings of the 1930's*, ed. Jack Salzman (New York: Pegasus, 1967).

"Thousand-Dollar Vagrant" was originally published in the *New Republic*, August 29, 1934, 67–69.

"I Want You Women up North to Know" was originally published in *Partisan Review* (March 1934): 4.

CPSIA information can be obtained
at www.ICGtesting.com
Printed in the USA
LVHW110637250123
737849LV00002B/357